Connections
Stories of East Asia

Connections
Stories of East Asia

David T. K. Wong

An Orchid Pavilion Book
Asia 2000 Limited
Hong Kong

© 2001 David T. K. Wong
All Rights Reserved

ISBN: 962–8783–05–X

An Orchid Pavilion Book
Published by Asia 2000 Ltd
Fifth Floor, 31A Wyndham Street
Central Hong Kong

http://www.asia2000.com.hk

Typeset in Adobe Garamond by Asia 2000 Ltd
Printed in Hong Kong by Editions Quaille

First Printing 2001

The rights of David T. K. Wong to be identified as the author of this work has been asserted in accordance with section 77 and 78 of the United Kingdom's Copyright Designs and Patents Act 1988.

This book is wholly a work of fiction and no reference is intended in it to any real person, living or dead. Some places and institutions are real, but any people associated with them are imagined. This book is sold subject to the condition that it shall not, by way of trade or otherwise, be lent, resold, hired out or otherwise circulated without the publisher's prior written consent in any form of binding or cover other than that in which it is published and without a similar condition including this condition being imposed on the subsequent purchaser.

To Friends

Who have enriched my life in more ways than I can recount

Contents

Crossing the Graveyard	9
The Card Index	23
The Colonel and the Professor	31
Foreigner's Rock	43
The English Secretary	57
Hand of Innocence	67
Aftershock	75
A Good Day for Dying	85
Lost River	93
Coil of the Serpent	107
Music From the Past	117
The Truth About Harry	125
Slow Poisons	135
Night Ferry From Macau	151
The Company House	167

Crossing the Graveyard

If Harmony and I had not risked the shortcut to school across the disused graveyard, Harmony might not have met with such a tragic end, and I would not have wandered the world with a dead crow sealed in a Jacob's biscuit tin. It has taken me more than twenty-five years to come to terms with my guilt and my sense of loss. Yesterday, I buried the poor crow at sea, together with my childhood fancies and awkward dreams.

Harmony and I were cousins, Harmony being older by three years. Our mothers were sisters who lived in a rundown neighbourhood on the outskirts of Malacca. Our homes were close to an enormous burial site, which, according to our mothers, had been used during previous centuries to bury murderers, traitors and outlaws. Because they had been evil creatures, their spirits were said to be capable of entering the bodies of the living to attack their internal organs.

Our mothers had little education. They adhered to a muddled form of Buddhism, which left scope for slaughtering chicken for dinner and blaming sorcerers and ghosts when things went wrong. Each kept at home a porcelain image of the Goddess of Mercy upon an altar, before whom they burnt joss-sticks and made offerings in return for protection against all things unseen. Each altar had a small red lamp kept permanently lit.

Their superstitions and fears accounted for the chilling tales they drummed into us. Our imaginations left us suitably frightened. We thus refrained from larking around the lichen-covered tombstones with older schoolmates.

Sinister dug-up holes, tall tropical grass, clumps of malacca palms, twisted banyans and a profusion of frangipani could be seen from the front and rear entrances to the graveyard. The last gave off a sweet, sickly smell that reminded us of Indian funerals. The frequent cawing of crows added a touch of eeriness.

Lessons in local history, however, taught us that those buried there were by no means as fearsome as our mothers had made out. The site was in fact first used in 1640 to bury some of the seven thousand people killed during the long siege of Portuguese Malacca by the Dutch. It fell into neglect when ninety per cent of the population fled after the Portuguese defeat. It was only after the British takeover in 1795 that the population slowly returned to its previous level.

In the meantime, the poor took to burying their dead there without let or hindrance. The British tried to impose order but were strapped for cash. It was the beginning of the twentieth century before a brick wall was built around the graveyard and a burial fee imposed.

After the Second World War the authorities decided to clear the site for redevelopment. But tracing descendants proved difficult due to the destruction of records during the Japanese occupation. So the project languished in a kind of limbo common in equatorial parts. Neither of us thought it productive to challenge our mothers with such facts. In any case, our new-found knowledge did not erase completely the prohibitions and fears etched into our psyches.

My mother died when I was nine and I went to live with Auntie Lan and Harmony. They occupied the front portion of the third floor of an old tenement. The rear housed a tailor and his family of five. The two parts were separated by a sturdy wooden partition. Our side was bright and airy because two large windows spanned the front of the building, offering a good view of our neighbourhood and a glimpse of the graveyard in the far distance. Auntie Lan's altar for the Goddess of Mercy was fixed to the wall between the two windows.

Auntie Lan was quite unlike my mother. She was jolly and robust whereas my mother, a washerwoman, was frail and timid. The most enduring feature about my mother was the rawness of her hands caused by the harsh soaps she used. They always felt so rough when she touched me. She also coughed a lot, often spitting up blood, and I only realized long afterwards that she had tuberculosis.

Auntie Lan ran an eatery in an evening food bazaar close to our homes and had a voice suitably muscular for the trade. She was expert at turning out all types of hawker dishes, like watercress seasoned with chili and fermented tofu, scrambled eggs with clams, and a wide variety of fried noodles. Her cooking had such a reputation that even the wealthiest in the town went out of their way to try her fare.

Harmony and I had been close even before I moved into her home. Many bonds bound us. The greatest was the secret discussions we had about our fathers. Neither of us had any recollection of them. Our mothers told us they were dead but snatches of overheard conversation led us to conclude that their statements were unreliable. Our fathers had merely vanished from our lives.

It became clear at a very young age that our mothers held jaundiced views about men in general and our fathers in particular. Auntie Lan was forever warning Harmony about men. She once said: "When you grow up you'll find out just how rotten they are. They'll say anything, promise anything, to get their way. The richer they are, the worse they are. You'll come to no good listening to them. They'll just use you as a plaything and then abandon you like garbage.

"Let me tell you a story my own mother told me about a girl who used to live in this town. She was a great beauty and her name was Azalea. Her father was a roadside cobbler. Her mother was from Cochin China and had mixed French and tribal blood.

"Azalea used to take the midday meal to her father at his pitch outside the office of the Eng Corporation. You've heard of the Engs. They've been here for generations and still dominate the tin mines, the rubber trade and many of the other businesses in this town.

"When Azalea was seventeen she caught the eye of the heir to the Eng fortune. The young man was so smitten he showered her and her family with presents. He even spoke of marriage.

"The rascal was quite engaging and Azalea was swept off her feet. Her parents were also overwhelmed. So they allowed the youngsters to keep company. The inevitable happened. Azalea got pregnant. It was then that the rascal showed his true colours. He claimed his father had forbidden their marriage because it could not be a marriage of equals. He offered money for an abortion instead. Azalea, however, would agree to nothing less than marriage and a proper place within the Eng household.

"Things were deadlocked. The poor cobbler and his family did not know what to do. When Azalea's condition could no longer be concealed, she went in the middle of the night to the front of the Eng mansion and hanged herself from a banyan tree. That, sad to say, is the fate of girls who lend their ears to silver-tongued men.

"At the funeral Azalea's mother cursed the Engs. She beseeched heaven and hell and all the gods known to her to destroy the Engs and end their progeny. But what was the use of that? Her beloved daughter was dead and to this day the Engs remain as powerful as ever. Where is justice in this world for the poor?"

Auntie Lan's story depressed Harmony and myself. Although we were not certain whether it was a true happening or just a legend, it dawned on us that our mothers might have been abandoned by our fathers as well. But we lacked the courage to probe.

After my mother died, Harmony provided the only company I had outside of school. We shared household chores, such as sweeping the floor and doing the laundry. We did our homework together and at night we spread straw mats before the altar and slept side by side.

Of course we engaged in horseplay and pillow fights like other children. But most of our spare time was spent trying to figure out the baffling behaviour of grown-ups and the whereabouts of our fathers. We swore we would find them some day. In the meantime we pledged to look after each other.

Neither of us saw much of Auntie Lan. When we left for school she would be still asleep. By the time we got home she would have left or be on the point of leaving to collect provisions for the evening's business. She did not finish her late trade till long after we had gone to sleep. Except for weekends, we only saw her briefly each day during dinner at the stall.

Weekends were the best of times. On Friday and Saturday we were allowed to help at the stall in the evening. That meant a chance for tips. We felt a certain pride when schoolmates and their families turned up and we would ask Auntie Lan to prepare their requirements with special care or to give them extra big helpings.

Our part of the tenement floor was sub-divided again after a fashion, by two seven-foot high mahogany wardrobes Auntie Lan salvaged from the discards of a departing colonial administrator. They stood side by side about eleven feet away from, but parallel to, the partitioning wall. Thus a small pen was formed to serve as Auntie Lan's bedroom. She slept on an old double bed with a brass bedstead.

A steel cable, fixed to nails in the partition wall at one end and to one of the wardrobes at the other, offered the means for a printed cotton curtain to be drawn across the enclosure.

Auntie Lan kept her things in one of the wardrobes. The other was used by Harmony and myself. The only item I had, however, apart from my clothes and my school things, was a Jacob's biscuit tin containing my birth certificate, some foreign stamps acquired from classmates, a pack of dog-eared playing cards and the few ringgits I had managed to save.

The area between the windows and the wardrobes was where Harmony and I spent most of our time. A square table with a Formica top and two metal folding chairs were the items most frequently called into service. We used them during breakfast, as well as for our homework. In order to hide the unsightliness of the backs of the wardrobes, we covered them with coloured pictures of foreign movie stars and a large calendar distributed by an American pharmaceutical company showing a scene of the Swiss Alps.

Our first venture across the graveyard happened when I was about eleven. We both got up late one morning because the sunlight, which normally woke us, had been blanketed by dark, threatening rain clouds. We leapt from our mats, dispensed with breakfast and raced for school. By the time we reached the graveyard wall, we knew we could not make it before the bell. The prospect of receiving demerits set our hearts pounding.

"Across the graveyard!" Harmony cried, suddenly, and started to race between the leprous tombstones. I ran after her, more out of fear of being left behind than anything else. We had previously learnt from schoolmates that cutting across the graveyard could save seven or eight minutes but we had never dared to chance it before.

To our relief, the shortcut enabled us not only to beat the bell but also the downpour that followed. We naturally maintained a conspiratorial silence before Auntie Lan. But something strange and frightening happened about three weeks later. I was awaken in the middle of the night by a noise. I opened my eyes to find Harmony missing from her mat. The light in Auntie Lan's enclosure was on. Though the drawn curtain I could make out silhouettes and hear whispering. Then I saw a patch of blood on Harmony's mat and I froze.

"Help Harmony quickly, Auntie Lan!" I yelled in panic. "The demons are after her! We went into the graveyard! I don't want her to die!" My mind was suddenly seized by visions of demons tearing at Harmony's entrails.

"You went into the graveyard, did you, you rascals?" Auntie Lan shouted from behind the curtain. "I'll deal with you tomorrow. Go back to sleep. Nothing's wrong with Harmony."

But I could not get back to sleep. I was covered with fear and confusion. I pretended to be asleep when Auntie Lan and Harmony came a short while later to clean the mat. After the light had been switched off again and Harmony was back on her mat, I reached over to take her hand. I suddenly realized she was the dearest person in the world to me and could not bear the thought of anything bad happening to her. But she flung my hand away, apparently upset over my betraying our secret.

The next afternoon, Auntie Lan was waiting for us when we got back from school. She was in an angry mood. "Haven't I told you not to go into the graveyard?" she demanded, giving each of us a clout across the back of our heads. "You like the company of the dead, do you? Then go and live in the graveyard! You think it's a joke? You could be inviting evil spirits into this very home. May the Goddess of Mercy have pity on us! I'll not have any more of that, you hear? If I catch you going there again, I'll give you the thrashings of your life."

We kept silent, took our punishments and looked suitably contrite. We knew from experience not to argue when Auntie Lan was angry. It was better to allow her to let off steam.

By evening, however, Harmony's annoyance with me had passed. She explained that crossing of the graveyard had nothing to do with her bleeding. It was just something girls had to go through on reaching a certain age.

"We're being educated and that means doing away with superstitions about ghosts and the like," Harmony said. "I don't want to live like my mother, full of fears about this and that and wasting her life cooped up in a lousy dump like this."

Though I conceded Auntie Lan's fears about demons and men might be exaggerated, the burial ground still gave me spooky feelings and I told Harmony I did not want to go through it again.

The next morning, when we were passing the graveyard on our way to school, Harmony grabbed me without warning by the arm and dragged me through the graveyard. She did that several more times in the days and weeks that followed. I resisted at first but I soon began to lose my uneasiness. The twisted banyans seemed less malevolent and the smell of the frangipani less sickly.

It gradually became our preferred route to and from school, in common with that of many of our classmates. We took pains to keep that from Auntie Lan, however.

Although our pattern of life seemed unaltered after breaking Auntie Lan's taboo, I knew something was definitely changing between Harmony and myself. For one thing, I was sprouting much faster than she. When I first came to live with Auntie Lan, I was three inches shorter than Harmony. But by the age of twelve, I was every bit as tall.

While I gained in height, Harmony fleshed out in all the places that mattered with girls. We used to engage in friendly wrestling matches to determine which of us should do the breakfast dishes or sweep the floors. Harmony used to beat me frequently. After I was twelve the outcome gradually became reversed, though I did not struggle too hard to break free from the headlocks she clamped on me. To have my face pressed against one of her burgeoning breasts was distinctly pleasurable. So too was the sensation when she straddled me to pin my shoulders to the floor for the regulation count of three.

I began noticing the glow in her face, the smooth perfection of her limbs and the almost regal manner in which she carried herself. So did the older boys at school and some of the customers at the food stall. I often caught them looking at her in a way I resented.

Harmony must have been aware of her own blossoming beauty, though she seemed not to mind others feasting their eyes on her. At home, when she drew the cotton curtain to change, I would invariable try to peep at her. If I caught sight of her partially naked I would feel an excruciating excitement.

The cousinly love I used to feel was being transformed in ways that were shameful and uncontrollable. I felt seared by a hot lava of guilt and base desires. I became terrified that a demon from the graveyard might indeed have turned me into a monster. But I could not talk about my condition to anybody, least of all to Harmony.

The months leading up to my thirteenth birthday were a period of unmitigated hell. I lost appetite and did poorly at school.

I often lay awake at night studying Harmony's sleeping form in the unnatural red glow of the altar lamp. I longed to pounce upon her, to embrace her and to smother her with kisses like the heroes of movies we had seen.

Harmony, noticing something amiss, often placed an arm around my shoulders — as she was accustomed to doing — to ask what the problem was. Her touch and the scent of her nearness only made matters worse. It was about all I could do to stop myself screaming. I felt I was slowly going out of my mind.

Following my thirteenth birthday, I drifted into a dull kind of melancholy, feeling at once foolish and expectant. But expectant of what I did not know. There seemed to be no future worth having without Harmony and no way of expressing my increasingly warped love for her. My studies deteriorated, and that was quickly noticed by both my teachers and Auntie Lan. But their stern warnings sounded like only peripheral noises around the screaming chaos in my soul.

One day, when making our journey across the graveyard, we noticed a crow prancing upon a headstone a short distance from the path we were taking. It was cawing loudly and flapping its wings. Though we thought its behaviour peculiar, we paid no attention. There were in any case a lot of crows in the neighbourhood.

On subsequent days, however, we noticed a crow behaving similarly upon the same headstone. We did not know whether it was the same creature but our curiosity was aroused. We went to examine the headstone. Inscribed upon it, in Chinese characters, were the name "Azalea" and a simple epitaph "Killed by Deceit".

I was astounded. It could only have been the grave of the Azalea Auntie Lan had spoken about. Questions buzzed around my head like hornets. Why was the crow drawing our attention to the grave? Was it some kind of omen? Or was the crow a reincarnation in the endless Buddhist cycles of rebirth? If so, was it of Azalea or her mother? In either case, what did it want from us? Did it expect us to avenge Azalea's death or what? I became truly frightened. I wanted no truck with the supernatural.

When I conveyed my fears to Harmony, she dismissed them out of hand. "You're getting as bad as Mother," she said. "There are no spirits or ghosts. They're just inventions of foolish people who cannot explain things they don't understand. This may or may not be the tomb of the Azalea of Mother's story. So what? If you searched among the thousands of tombstones you are bound to find an Azalea or two. What then? The silly crow hopping around is probably just a coincidence."

Shortly afterwards I began having a recurring nightmare about a crow revealing itself as a reincarnation of Azalea's mother seeking vengeance. I felt as if I was being sucked into that ancient tragedy. But given Harmony's skepticism, I kept my nightmares to myself.

Then, one Friday evening, a group of well-dressed young men turned up our stall at the bazaar. They appeared flushed and florid with drink. Harmony attended to them and they began ogling her in a disrespectful way.

Their leader was a short, podgy man who kept flashing a greasy smile. He had an unusually thick set of eyebrows, which somehow appeared abbreviated, as if their ends had been chopped off. That lent his face a shifty quality.

The group ate their meal boisterously and upon settling up its leader gave Harmony a tip of five ringgits. That was extremely generous in those days, for that amounted to almost the cost of the meal itself.

The next evening the young man with the strange eyebrows came back alone, in a gleaming Italian sports car. He parked within sight of the stall. He was more subdued than the previous evening but boasted that his car was the only one of its kind in Malacca. He lingered after his meal to engage Harmony in conversation. He again tipped her five ringgits.

When he turned up the following weekend as well, I began to resent him. Perhaps I envied his smartly tailored shirts, his immaculate white trousers and his stylish two-tone shoes, not to mention his sports car, which was certainly worthy of admiration and respect. He ordered noodles costing little more than fifty sens but again left a tip of five ringgits. I was convinced he was up to no good and I told Harmony so.

"What have you got against him?" Harmony asked.

"Just look at his eyebrows! They mark him as a man not to be trusted," I replied.

"He's just a customer and he hasn't tried anything funny. He's a bit chatty but what's wrong with that? I don't have my mother's fear of men, even when they have strange eyebrows. He's just returned from studying business administration in America. It would be useful to know people like that, especially when it comes to looking for a job. He seems well connected. He may even be able to help us find our fathers."

What Harmony said seemed reasonable. Reflection told me that my dislike for the man was rooted in jealousy, though I could hardly say that to Harmony. My preoccupation with my rival produced an unexpected effect, however. It took my mind off my nightmares.

The man kept coming back, weekend after weekend, and I could sense him gaining Harmony's confidence. I was gripped by a feeling of impending disaster, of somehow losing Harmony altogether.

Then one Saturday evening the man hung around till after the rush of the dinner trade. As Harmony and I were about to go home, he asked if Harmony would like to take a spin in his car.

I could see Harmony being tempted. I immediately pulled her to one side and whispered: "Don't go with him! You don't even know his name. You can't be too careful these days. He may be a white slave trader or an underworld character. Don't be taken in by his big tips and his fancy car."

"Don't be so melodramatic," Harmony said. "You've been reading too many bad comics."

"Why else would he leave such big tips? He is using them to get on the good side of you, to buy his way into your confidence."

"Do you think I care about his tips?" Harmony retorted, angrily. "I enjoy talking to the guy, if you must know, because he's been places and can tell me what they're like. We haven't been anywhere, not even as far as Johore Bahru, let alone New York and Hollywood. I'll split his tips with you if that's what's bothering you!"

My inability to persuade Harmony about the nature of the customer left me frustrated. "Keep your lousy money. I'm not so easily bought!" I cried, rashly, desperate to make her see sense.

"If that's what you think then I might as well go and enjoy my ride!"

That was the first time Harmony and I had ever quarrelled. I had not meant to hurt her. I was just worried about her being compromised. As I watched them drive away, a terrible foreboding descended upon me.

When I got home I tossed and turned on my mat, oppressed as if the weight of the world was crushing the breath out of me. I wanted to make up with Harmony and longed for her return. But she never came back. Neither did Auntie Lan, until well into Sunday morning.

Auntie Lan was hysterical on arriving home. It appeared she had spent the night at the morgue. Harmony had been killed in a car crash. My heart almost stopped upon hearing the news.

Days of blurred agony followed. The newspapers reported that the car had gone off the road and smashed into a tree. It had been driven by none other than Eng Kok-king, the heir to the Eng fortune. Harmony was killed instantly but the driver survived for a few days.

It came out during the inquest that in his delirium Eng Kok-king kept crying out about a woman and a child appearing suddenly in front of the car. He crashed trying to avoid them. However, witnesses on the spot reported no sign of any woman or child.

Auntie Lan became a changed woman after the tragedy. She lost interest in her stall. She kept kneeling before the Goddess of Mercy, beating her head on the floor and lamenting: "Why my baby, oh Goddess of Mercy? What have I done in my previous existence to deserve this? How did my baby come to be in a car with an Eng? My baby hasn't hurt a soul. She was a good girl. Why rob her of life?"

I was no less devastated but I had to mask my true feelings. I could not tell Auntie Lan that we had been crossing the graveyard regularly, that we had found the grave of Azalea and that I had quarrelled with Harmony before her ride. I was consumed by guilt. If I had not provoked Harmony, she might not have taken that fatal ride.

Strangely, the deaths of Harmony and Eng Kok-king brought an abrupt end of my nightmares. I became more convinced than ever their deaths had to be connected in an unfathomable way to Azalea and the Eng of an earlier generation.

As the days of misery went by, I felt unaccountably drawn to Azalea's grave, as if an irresistible force was beckoning. I went there accordingly, and to my amazement I found a dead crow next to the headstone.

The discovery set me trembling. Supernatural spirits had to be at work. If the spirit of Azalea had previously resided in the crow, where was she now? Had she been reincarnated into something else? What of Harmony? Had she been reborn and, if so, where could I find her?

A hundred such questions whirled around my brain. I quickly put the dead crow into my school satchel and took it home, in the hope that the carcass might provide answers to such conundrums. In order not to upset Auntie Lan, I hid the dead crow in my Jacob's biscuit tin and examined it when I was alone. But it shed no light on my concerns. When it started to smell, I took the tin to a tinsmith and had the lid welded tight.

The loss of Harmony and the uncertain fate hanging over me sent me into deep depression. The unceasing lamentations of Auntie Lan made matters worse. I speculated whether, with Harmony gone, the unrequited dead might reach out for me. I felt I had to escape. So I ran off to sea, taking with me the dead crow in my Jacob's biscuit tin. That was the last I saw of Auntie Lan.

I have since travelled the world, from Haiti to Hokkaido, from Mozambique to New Orleans. I have witnessed voodoo rituals, delved into shamanistic practices and listened to countless tales of ghostly happenings and supernatural interventions. But I have yet to come across an occult thesis, which unambiguously supports or dismisses a possible linkage between the deaths of Azalea and Harmony.

Last week, the steamer I was working on collided at night with a small native fishing craft while passing through the Straits of Malacca. That necessitated an unscheduled stop at the port itself. The unexpected return to the scene of my childhood brought back with all my old longings and pain. It also set me wondering whether that collision had been due to pure chance.

Mercifully, since the stay in port was brief, no shore leave was permitted. Though I realized that I could never be completely rid of the bitter sweet memories of my youth, the collision brought home to me the prudence of ridding myself of vestiges from the past. For all I knew they might be capable of transmitting secret signals for creatures of the nether world to track me down. That was why I decided to bury the poor crow at sea yesterday, in my battered Jacob's biscuit tin.

The Card Index

Piao looked down upon Yin-yin lying spread-eagled upon their double bed. Her glossy black hair was spread like a dark halo around her head while her face registered a strange, wide-eyed look of surprise. There was something classical and beautiful about her features, Piao thought. With her clear brow, high cheek bones and fine pointed chin, she had what the Chinese would describe as a "melon-seed" face. But there was also something vaguely cold and mean about her. It was an impression conveyed by a certain hardness in her eyes and by the way her mouth pulled scornfully downwards at the corners.

She scorned him even in death, Piao thought. His gentle brown eyes blinked in disbelief behind his horn-rimmed spectacles. Could he really have killed her, he wondered, as he turned his back on the corpse and sat down at the foot of the bed. His wife's feet seemed to point up accusingly at him. She had small, dainty feet, with elegantly shaped toes. He noticed for the first time her toenails had been painted a brilliant red. They were quite attractive, and he wondered whether they had only recently been painted or whether he had just been blind to them before.

Around his own feet lay what remained of his precious card index. He had kept his cards neatly housed in a series of shoeboxes for the past twenty years or more. Since his marriage they had been kept under the bed, much to the irritation of his wife. Now the shoeboxes were heaped in a sorry pile in a corner of the room, their contents spewed all over the floor.

They must be hopelessly mixed up in terms of sources, chronology and subject, he thought. He bent down and picked up a card at random. Upon it, recorded in his own neat handwriting, was an extract from one of the special chapters in the Twenty-Four Dynastic Histories dealing with relations with foreign countries. He allowed the card to drop back on to the floor and picked up another. This one contained an extract from *Geographia Universalis* by Sebastian Munster, published in 1540. Were such extracts from ancient tomes, no matter how laboriously acquired, really worth killing to preserve, he wondered, soothing out lovingly the creases where the card had been stepped upon.

Piao scratched his thinning hair absent-mindedly. He felt mildly surprised, even now, over his ability to kill. He turned his hands over and examined them carefully. They did not appear to be the hands of a killer. They looked frail and thin and wanting in strength, and yet they were the hands that had just taken the life of his wife. He did not consider himself a violent man, far from it. All his life he had shied away from conflict. Indeed, if anything, he had been too ready to accept bullying, too willing to seek compromise. So what had made him break away from the established habits of a lifetime? He had once read somewhere that the more educated a person became, the more restricted would be his range of actions. He was not only educated but a schoolteacher besides, as were his father and grandfather before him. If that theory held true he should be almost incapable of violence. Could there really be more of a beast lurking within each man than moral upbringing and education could ever tame?

It had all happened so suddenly. That Sunday morning had begun in the usual fashion. After breakfast he had walked his twelve-year-old daughter and his ten-year-old son to Sunday school as had been his practice for years. He was not a Christian. Neither was his wife, but she had their children baptized to gain readier admittance to the exclusive missionary schools attended by the children of her rich friends and relatives.

He had not liked that conversion of convenience but had not objected, for the sake of matrimonial peace, and had not minded his weekly task of taking the children to and from Sunday school. At least the mile-long walk afforded him the chance to get out of their small flat and enjoy a smoke. He was fond of his pipe but normally smoked only at school because Yin-yin objected to smoking in the flat. If he felt a particular urge for a pipe at home, he would take a walk around the neighbourhood to gratify his need.

Upon his return from taking his children to Sunday school he had found Yin-yin in the process of cleaning their room, and he had been shocked to see his cards scattered all over the floor and being trampled underfoot by his wife. For one traumatic moment he saw everything dear to him being defiled and threatened with destruction. But before he could even express his anguish Yin-yin had assailed him in that irritable tone of voice to which he had grown accustomed: "I'm sick of your cluttering up the place with your junk! Sick! Sick! Sick! Do you hear? I've burned half of your damned cards already. I want you to put the rest of them in the kitchen stove. I'm not going to have those boxes around to breed cockroaches any longer."

He saw her then as the tormentor who had demeaned his life, as someone standing for everything atavistic and unenlightened in society, and in one wild, uncontrollable surge of anger he had strangled her.

Reflecting upon his deed, Piao felt neither regret nor alarm, only a weary indifference mingled with a slight sense of the ridiculous. He would never be able to explain at his trial why he had killed his wife. It would have been different if he had killed her because he had caught her in bed with a lover. Then it would be a crime of passion within the understanding of ordinary mortals and no further explanation would be necessary. But a killing caused by the destruction of some filing cards would be incomprehensible. How could he explain the meaning they held for him? How could people see them as he did, as his individual quest for truth and knowledge and fulfilment? He would never be able to explain to his children either. They would both probably think him quite mad.

He decided there and then that he would offer no explanation to the police. Let the prosecutor come up with theories on motives at his trial. He would say nothing. In the absence of a convincing motive, the court might yet spare him the death sentence. They might just lock him up. In that case, there might still exist the possibility of reconstructing his card index in the solitude of his confinement. The prospect gave his spirits a lift.

He had begun his card index while still at university. During his studies he had come across a reference to Augustus the Strong, Elector of Saxony and King of Poland, trading a whole regiment of dragoons with the King of Prussia for a set of vases made during the Kang Hsi period at the famous kilns of Ching-te Chen. The fact that a foreign ruler could display such appreciation for a piece of alien artistry had caused him to ponder the strange interconnections of human destiny. It had left him wondering whether the destiny of Poland or Europe had been affected in any material way by that exchange. Certainly the Roman craving for Chinese silk, especially during the reigns of Hadrian and the Antonines, had altered the history of the Roman Empire. It had contributed significantly towards its economic and moral decline. If the Chinese had not from the earliest time regarded the manufacture of silk as a state secret and any attempt to take silkworms or eggs out of the country as a crime punishable by death, the whole history of Western civilization might have been different.

The thought had occurred to him then that the traditional approach to history was thoroughly unsatisfactory. History segmented into the irrelevancies of reigns and dynasties might make for the narrow glorification of a particular race or nation but it would be less than adequate in recounting the broad flow of human destiny. It would not account for all the fateful twists and turns caused by fundamental breakthroughs in art or science or ideas nor the large and unpredictable consequences arising out of some spontaneous and innocent craving, be it for silk or spices or whatever.

How different the world would be if gunpowder or paper had never been invented or if Einstein's theory of relativity had never been enunciated. To trace the roots of each human advance and to present a world perspective of its effect would pose enormous problems of scholarship. But if someone could bring it off he might establish for himself a name more respected than that of Gibbon or Ssuma Ch'ien.

The attraction of the prospect gradually took such a hold on him that he wrote a number of papers reflecting that approach. They met with a measure of approval from his professors and that had been enough for him to start his card index.

That secret ambition, once whetted, grew into an obsession which stayed with him even after his graduation and marriage. He never told Yin-yin about it, however, for he was afraid of being ridiculed. He knew she was not one to understand the stuff of dreams. She had come from a banker's family and her approach to life was coldly practical. Even before their marriage she had suggested careers for him in commerce or high finance. One had to make the most of one's connections, she had told him. But the pursuit of wealth held little attraction for him. His material needs had always been modest, and he knew no career in the commercial world could offer as much satisfaction as his researches in history. So, uncharacteristically, he had stood firm against the pressures from Yin-yin and had settled, to her intense disappointment, for the safe but impecunious vocation of a history teacher.

He had every intention of making up for her disappointment by being a good and considerate husband. But philosophically they belonged to different worlds.

For him, to be able to trace the effects the Nisacan horses of Central Asia had on the destiny of empires would be like an exciting journey of discovery. Those horses had been so sturdy they could go into battle fully protected by heavy chain-mail and yet carry an armoured warrior. They had enabled China to check the advance of the Hsiungnu nomads, and it had been the desire to obtain such horses that had caused Emperor Wu to allow regular trade to be maintained with Persia. Because alfalfa was such an important item in their diet, that had caused the grass to be planted in China. The horses had been so magnificent that even Alexander the Great turned aside from his preoccupations to see them. And so the tentacles of causation stretched out from the steppes of Central Asia to affect the affairs of nations far and wide.

But unfortunately, such dusty revelations, so painstakingly pieced together, meant nothing to Yin-yin. For her excitement took more the form of a new fur coat or a mention in the social columns for attending some gala function. But how much of that sort of excitement could a man afford on a teacher's salary? He soon discovered, like others before him, that love and good intentions were not sufficient to sustain a marriage. So gradually they became estranged and before long the nagging began.

At the beginning he made a point of not answering back, partly because he wanted to mollify his wife and partly because he wanted to buy peace through silence. But Yin-yin merely took his silence as a retreat and nagged all the more.

On one occasion, when he was deeply engrossed in making extracts for his card index from a book borrowed from the university library, Yin-yin had upbraided him with unusual vehemence.

"Just look at you!" she had scoffed. "The president of the Students Union who was going to set the world on fire! What a laugh! Can't you do anything except bury your nose in a book?"

"I'm doing something constructive. I'm trying to get a better understanding of history," he had replied.

"A fat lot of good that will do, when we cannot even afford a servant!"

On another occasion, in sheer bewilderment over another of Yin-yin's outburst, he had demanded in exasperation: "What do you expect of me? Haven't I been a decent husband? I've tried to provide for the family as best I can. I haven't any of the traditional vices. I don't drink or gamble or take drugs or womanize. I don't stay out till all hours of the night like the husbands of some of your friends. So what more do you want? All I ask is some peace to read. Is that too much to ask?"

"Oh, you're just so dull! You really bore me. I don't know why I ever married you."

Only then did he realize that dullness constituted some sort of matrimonial failing. He accepted the indictment and thereafter kept silent more than ever. But the scoldings continued. Gradually he got accustomed to them, in much the same way one got used to a recurring noise.

As the children grew up he found consolation in entertaining them with historical anecdotes of one sort or another, such as the story of conjurors sent to China by the Parthian king, Mithradates II, or that of the Byzantine Emperor Justinian persuading Nestorian monks to smuggle silkworm eggs out of China in hollowed-out staves.

Piao thus reviewed the odd fragments of his life with Yin-yin with a quiet melancholy. What a mess they had made of it. Even their lovemaking, that ultimate cement for poor marriages, had turned into a war of attrition waged with dry loins. If it had not been for the children it would have been kinder to liberate themselves from each other. But he had never imagined liberation would take so unexpected a form.

Suddenly, Piao was shaken out of his reverie by the sound of Yin-yin's voice calling from the kitchen. "Where are those damned cards I told you to bring out? I still have to cook lunch, you know. I haven't got all day."

"Coming, dear," Piao replied. He gathered up a pile of his index cards lovingly and carried them to the kitchen like a sacrifice.

"The Card Index" has appeared in *PEN International* in Britain and *The Peak* magazine in Hong Kong. It has also been broadcast by Radio Television Hong Kong in Hong Kong.

The Colonel and the Professor

The fateful hour, the hour without shadows, was fast approaching and the atmosphere was alive with tension. The chanted slogans of the last three days had been replaced by a low, menacing murmur, like the growling of some lurking beast. The tranquil pagodas, glistening crimson and gold under the punishing sun, provided an incongruous backdrop to the unfolding drama between stern-faced soldiers with G-3 automatic rifles and the massed citizenry of the capital demanding an end to the Junta.

The Colonel, dressed in battle fatigues, was filled with bitterness as he surveyed the crowds from behind barricades around the parliament building. He had a stiff, military bearing, reinforced by a brooding concentration born of the habit of command. His dark eyes flashed angrily between his high-boned cheeks and his mouth, normally gentle and attractive, was compressed in frustration. He focused his field glasses on the multitudes gathered seventy yards or so beyond the barbed wire perimeter and cursed under his breath.

The crowds had swollen to over three hundred thousand, perhaps even four, during the last three days, as if sheer numbers could secure for them what had long been denied. They stretched as far as the eye could see, jostling high-spiritedly across roads and pavements, waving from balconies and windows, huddling expectantly on rooftops and every other vantage point.

They seemed oblivious of the sweltering heat preceding the monsoons. They simply waited for the noon hour set by their leaders for breaking their fast and marching on parliament, anxious to participate in a great historic event even if only as witnesses. In their innocence, they expected to topple the Junta by storming the parliament. Some of the demonstrators clutched portraits of ancient heroes and martyrs in remembrance of past sacrifices. Others displayed emblems of universities and civic associations. A great many wore red or white headbands inscribed with reckless commitments to success. A forest of flags, placards and banners trumpeted their demands. Freedom, democracy and an end to corruption and dictatorship!

How naive they were, the Colonel thought, exasperated. Had they learnt nothing from the bloodbaths staining the history of their country over the past thirty years? Did they really think the Junta cared about people shouting slogans? He pitied all the well-meaning people gathered in front of him, monks in saffron robes, doctors and nurses in hospital gowns, lawyers in judicial dress, children in school uniforms, businessmen, hawkers, film actresses, peasants, housewives, trishaw drivers, junior civil servants and the rest. Most of all he pitied the Professor, his respected friend and former teacher, for leading so many to certain disaster. The Junta could never be dislodged by mere demonstrations.

It had been fortuitous that the protest had not been suppressed already. A visit by the head of a European government to sign an arms supply agreement had caused the Junta to stay its hand. It could not afford to embarrass one of the few remaining countries still prepared to turn a blind eye to its record of abuses. But now that the dignitary and his entourage were safely out of the way, it was ready to act. A dawn to dusk curfew had already been proclaimed as a prelude to more drastic action. But the crowds, embolden by a false scent of victory, had chosen to ignore it.

They would soon pay the price, the Colonel thought, for there would be no safety in numbers. The larger the protest, the more ruthless the response. He dreaded the massacre to come.

The Colonel and the Professor

"Unsavory and lawless elements must be taught a lesson. Shoot all curfew breakers," the Junta had decreed.

The Colonel was well aware of what the Bren guns mounted on armoured personnel carriers and the automatic rifles cradled by his men were capable of. What a carnage it would be! He felt sick to the stomach and silently cursed the Professor and his associates for placing him in such an impossible position. They had upset his own deep laid plans and left him teetering on the edge of disaster.

He had been so patient, so careful, so wary of the secret police and spies planted everywhere. For years he had sought out the most onerous commands, enduring the hardships at primitive border regions just to avoid brutalizing unarmed students and civilians. Lest fellow officers mistook his manoeuvrings for greed — because the pickings from smugglers and opium traders in the border areas were rich indeed — he made a point of passing on the "taxes" and "fees" to his superiors.

His successes in pacifying bandits and insurgents and his regular tributes soon caught the eye of the Junta. The generals began accepting him as one who knew how to play the game. As a consequence he rose rapidly through the ranks and his recent appointment to a command in the capital had placed him within an ace of the real levers of power. It was just his luck to have to deal at once with the largest mass protest the city had ever seen. That threw him right into the firing line. He either had to do the dirty work of the Junta or see the ruin of his plans.

The Colonel searched for the Professor through his field glasses and spotted him sitting on a straw mat under a large umbrella. Like the other leaders, he was dressed in a white shirt and a white sarong. His eyes were closed and his face serene. He seemed to be holding up well in spite of three days on nothing but glucose and water. He was sitting cross-legged, with his delicate hands resting comfortably upon his thighs and his fingers curled in the traditional posture of meditation. He looked older and thinner but otherwise still exuded that old aura of moral authority.

Poor loveable dreamer, the Colonel thought. He should have gone into a monastery to become an arhat, passing his days intoning sutras and fingering prayer beads. Instead, he had to involve himself in the rotten business of politics. He had always been too naive and trusting, too ready to believe in man's capacity for reason and compassion. He should have lived during the legendary age of philosopher kings and not when more and more of mankind was falling under the yoke of the likes of the Junta.

The Colonel remembered the Professor declaring during one of his lectures: "Napoleon, though a military genius, once held there were only two powers in the world — the sword and the mind. He concluded that ultimately the mind always conquered the sword, because of the mind's ability to renew indefinitely such human ideals as freedom, justice, courage and compassion, against which the sword is helpless. A sword can only kill people, not ideals, and given enough time swords will rust.

"Therefore, though the age seems benighted, do not despair. Rule by the sword cannot endure because it lacks legitimacy. It will collapse eventually from its own moral decay. There is no need to take up arms. Peaceful and steadfast resistance is enough. Remember we are Buddhists. The use of violence is a sin, not to mention the taking of life. Besides, the means we use are every bit as important as the ends we seek. Evil methods breed evil in their users, even when used against evil men."

There had been a time when the Professor's words found resonance with his own inclinations. They had shared a common upbringing, although a generation separated them. Their education, by tradition, required spending several weeks a year in monasteries, serving monks, reciting sutras, begging for food and learning humility and compassion. Buddhism and the contemplative life seemed ideally suited to their gentle and easy-going race. Indeed, there was still a part of him which longed to live in tune with the seasons, to enjoy the abundance of nature and to find contentment in a begging bowl! But that sort of life became increasingly unthinkable under the Junta.

For a time he thought it a mere aberration, caused by the ineptitudes and bickerings of politicians and by a people unbalanced by the temptation of material things. The Junta would fade away once things got back on an even keel. Instead he saw the media brought increasingly under control and foreign journalists expelled. A puppet parliament was installed to lend an air of legality to the Junta's every wish. Then the repression and the killings began. Those suspected of opposing the whittling away of freedoms were rounded up, many never to be seen again. After two of his best friends had been beaten to death for writing satirical verses in a university magazine, he judged it necessary to oppose the Junta by fair means or foul.

It baffled him how, after all that had happened around the world, the Professor could remain so firm in his belief in the essential goodness of man. Man had to be judged by his actions and what had man brought about in the last hundred years?

Two World Wars and countless lesser ones. Nazi gas chambers and Communist labour camps. Regimes everywhere murdering in the name of patriotism and justifying lies on orders from the state. Bombs capable of laying waste to whole cities and missiles capable of delivering them half a world away. Instruments of slaughter bartered for profit or political favours. Populations decimated for the sake of oil, a sphere of influence or some petty mercantile advantage. Hatreds stirred up because of differences in race, colour, caste or creed. Food routinely destroyed in accordance with "market economics" while people starved elsewhere. Tyranny, cynicism, inhumanity and greed spreading everywhere like uncontrollable diseases.

No, he could not remain optimistic. Each day that passed saw the sword enhancing itself with machine guns, tanks and all manner of weaponry. Its obscene triumphs, in the form of blasted bodies, severed limbs, walking skeletons and mangled corpses, bludgeoned the world through newspaper pages and television screens.

Against that how could the mind prevail? It could only be numbed by a surfeit of horrors and drugged by self-interest and greed. If Napoleon's dictum had once been true, it was now — like Euclidean geometry — obsolete. He saw mankind slipping inexorably into a new dark age. If man had to return to living by the sword, then let him wield it with a measure of justice and fairness. It was that belief that had driven him to enlist in the army.

Yet, years of killing bandits and criminals, sinning against his religion and putting up with unthinkable excesses, were about to come to naught. His stratagems and plottings had only brought him face to face with a blank wall!

"Message from Headquarters, Sir," a Major came up and reported. "We can start action. The main routes have been sealed and reserves are in position. Are we to act before the march?"

The Major had the dull, unimaginative face of a peasant, but the Colonel knew him to be a loyal and reliable soldier.

"There's a lot of them," the Colonel replied. "We don't want to be hasty. Although we have fire power, the Chinese have a saying: Even an elephant can be overwhelmed by ants, if there are enough of them."

"There's no fear of that, Sir. They're not like the rascals at the frontiers. They have no heart for a fight. The first volley will have them scattering like frightened rabbits."

"The Professor must not be harmed. Our orders are to take him for a treason trial. He is too well known internationally and it will go down badly if he gets killed."

"We can shoot into the wings, away from the ringleaders."

"No, the Professor may still get trampled in the panic. Let me try a ruse. I used to know him quite well. I'll go and talk to him. That will separate him from his followers. I can then grab him before anyone knows what's happening. Have a platoon ready to bring him in when I signal."

"But, Sir, that's dangerous! You'll be very exposed. What if something goes wrong? They are getting smarter. Some now carry slings and stones. You may get hit by a rock or bottle. It will be worse if they get their hands on you. You'll be torn apart!"

"That's a risk I'll have to take. Broadcast another warning that curfew breakers will be severely dealt with. If anything does go wrong, you're in command."

"Yes, Sir!"

The Colonel removed the field glasses from around his neck and picked up a loud hailer. The armpits of his fatigues were already stained with sweat and a fine film of perspiration dampened his brow. As he stepped from behind the barricades his body was stiff and tense, for he dreaded the massacre that was on the cards. He had only one chance in a million of averting it and that depended on the Professor.

He knew the troops would have no compunction about shooting. They had been too well indoctrinated. Their religious scruples and human instincts had been systematically expunged. The Junta had taken simple peasant lads and elevated them into a privileged class. It had paid them better than the rest of the population and plied them with imported luxuries at a fraction of their market value. Officers enjoyed "extras" in the form of permits and licences for their families and relatives. Regional commanders got cuts in the income from illegal logging and other contraband trades. Soldiers were encouraged to rape, pillage and kill during missions, partly to terrorize opponents and partly to bind their destinies to that of the Junta. Once they had committed atrocities, their fates and those of their masters became inextricably linked.

The Colonel recalled the attempts to indoctrinate officers at the elite Defence Services Academy. A British lecturer had been used for the purpose, a gentleman with a superior way of speaking through his nose. He had expounded on law and order being a primary responsibility of the state, something to be maintained at all cost. Once a state failed to provide security for its citizens and their property, it would forfeit its mandate to rule, the lecturer had declared.

The Colonel smiled ironically in recollection. It had all sounded plausible enough at the time. He now wondered whether that British expert had ever confronted three hundred thousand angry citizens and whether he considered shooting them a fitting way of ensuring their security.

After the Colonel had moved thirty yards into no man's land, he called on his loud hailer. "I am the commanding officer. I would like to talk to the Professor." His announcement was greeted by a chorus of abuse and some scattered rocks and stones. But the missiles fell wide of the mark.

"Professor, this is Nyi," the Colonel continued, ignoring the initial response. "It is important that I talk to you."

After a brief interval there was a stirring among the ranks of the demonstrators and eventually someone assisted a frail white figure unsteadily to his feet.

As the Professor moved forward slowly, with an uplifted arm to curb further missiles, an eerie hush descended. After the Professor had travelled twenty yards, the Colonel dropped his loud hailer and moved briskly to narrow the remaining distance between them, in full awareness that every step he took increased his danger. When he met up with his old friend he placed his palms together and lifted them to his forehead in traditional greeting and the Professor reciprocated.

"Is it really you, Nyi?" the Professor asked with a smile. "It is good to see you again after so long. I thought you were up-country."

"I have just been assigned here. I'm sorry not to have called to pay my respects," the Colonel said, removing his helmet as a gesture of respect and as an indication to the demonstrators of his peaceful intentions. His hair was stiff and closely cropped and there was an anxious and haunted look in his eyes. "There is not much time, Professor. You must ask your people to disperse."

The Professor smiled again. "Is that your uniform speaking, my dear boy? Since when have we been divided into your people and my people? Are we not one people?"

"I'm sorry. I didn't mean it that way. You must trust me and get the people to leave. Quickly, but without causing panic."

"I cannot. They are all worked up, united as they have never been before. In five minutes they will march on the parliament. They mean to put an end of the tortures and the killings once and for all. Even the Junta must realize this is not a protest by a handful of students. It is a display of universal disapproval. There are similar protests in a dozen provincial towns. Even the most evil of men must retain a shred of conscience and human decency. They must see they are not wanted and should leave rather than spill more blood."

"You do not know the generals as I do. They rule by the sword and can only be removed by the sword."

The Professor sighed. "The sword! It is always the sword. That has already been tried and what has that achieved? Cycles of killings as unalterable as our cycles of rebirth. Successes with the sword can only arouse passion and lead to more bloodshed. There must come a time for killings to stop, for forgiveness and reconciliation to be given a chance. If sinners see no hope of redemption, what else is there for them to look forward to?"

"This is not the time for moral philosophy. You must abandon the march. Please get the people to disperse while there's still time. Avoid the main thoroughfares. They have already been blocked. Use the side lanes. The Junta means business. I have orders to shoot."

"What has happened to the man I used to know, Nyi, the one who once harboured such lofty dreams? Would he shoot me also without a qualm? I cannot believe he has thrown in his lot so completely with the Junta."

"You know I will never do that. But there is no time to explain. The people must leave at once or thousands will die."

"Not even the Junta can contemplate a massacre on such a scale, in the heart of the capital, in broad daylight. There are holy monks and abbots among us, women and children. Join us, Nyi, to end the torment of our nation, for the good of our people. Tell your men to lay down their arms and the nightmare will be over."

"I wish it were that simple. My men will obey no such order. They know what they're here to do. They will shoot to kill."

"The Junta can't kill everybody in the capital."

"Not everybody, but enough to cow the population. The streets will run red with blood. I promise you the soldiers will shoot. I beg you to disperse before it's too late."

A bewildered look came into the Professor's eyes, as if he could not believe his ears. He searched desperately in the Colonel's face for some hint, some shadow of reassurance, it was only a nightmare. But the Colonel's serious demeanor confirmed the truth of what he had said.

"Merciful Buddha! What have I done?" the Professor cried. "How can they disperse? The streets are packed!"

"Do your best. I will hold off action as long as I can. Trust me. I'll explain everything later."

Suddenly the Professor swayed and raised a hand to his brow. "I think I'm going to faint," he gasped.

The Colonel grabbed the Professor by the arm and shook him roughly. "No!" he hissed through clenched teeth. "You can't faint! You must go back to get them to disperse!"

But the Professor was already slumping towards the ground. As the Colonel picked him up, he saw a number of protestors hurrying forward. A tight knot of tension gathered in the pit of his stomach. Even without a backward glance he knew a platoon was already racing towards him. All he had to do was to make for the safety of the soldiers with the Professor. In a matter of seconds he would be covered in glory and his own scheme for power would come closer to realization.

But he could not do that. Although the bloodletting could not be stopped for the present, one day it would have to stop, if there was to be hope for his tormented land. He realized at the same time that his way forward would only perpetuate rule by the sword. There would be no other way of satisfying the thirst for revenge and for settling debts of blood. Was it possible that only someone as impossibly idealistic as the Professor stood a chance of taming the sword?

It was a slim chance but the only one on offer for healing the wounds of the nation. So thinking, he ran towards the demonstrators carrying the frail old man, yelling the while: "Run! Run! They're going to shoot!"

Even as he ran he heard the rattle of automatic fire.

"The Colonel and the Professor" has appeared in *Short Story International* in the United States and has been broadcast by the British Broadcasting Corporation on Radio 4 in Britain and by Radio Eire in Ireland.

Foreigner's Rock

The anchor clung like a grotesque insect upon the prow as the white painted liner edged alongside. Passengers crowded the decks in spite of the fierce tropical sunshine. They were in high spirits, drinking in the faded charm of the betel nut island of Penang, one of the original trading posts of the British East India Company. On the pier a motley collection of immigration officials, shipping functionaries, tourist guides and stevedores made ready to carry out their divers duties.

Four weeks into their world cruise, the passengers had grown accustomed to tossing streamers, blowing hooters and waving to complete strangers. Having paid good money, they felt entitled to their fun.

Krishna watched their antics with a wry smile. His cotton shirt and drill trousers, immaculately starched and ironed, were photic in their whiteness. They contrasted sharply with the almost negrito blackness of his skin. He had wavy black hair, dark flashing eyes and sensual nostrils. But it was his fleshy mouth, dimpling superciliously at the corners that gave him the aspects of an arrogant Hindu god, seemingly possessed with the power to play havoc with feminine hearts.

But being twenty-seven, the father of two children and still stuck as a guide with Paradise Tours weighed upon Krishna. What a way to earn a living, he thought, as he waited for the gangplank to be heaved into place. He held a placard in one hand, ready for display. Written upon it in bold capitals were the words "Mrs. Jodie Hamilton".

He wondered what specimen of American womanhood he was to be lumbered with. This one was supposed to be a widow from Dallas, Texas, travelling alone, and apparently so lacking in commonsense as to sign up for the exorbitant seven-day deluxe tour of the island.

He had an antipathy towards American women, particularly those arriving on luxury liners. It was an aversion shaped by eight years of misplaced hopes and cruel disappointments. They never turned out as he had imagined, like the beauties in Hollywood films or the uninhibited hippies roasting themselves silly on the remoter beaches.

Instead, they came over-fed and over-aged, too ready to be thrilled by bigness and awed by antiquity. But it was their emotional and sexual untidiness he particularly disliked. They seemed to expect every casual liaison to turn into some grand passion, though — truth to tell — he had often exploited their confusion to his own financial advantage.

He wondered whether Mrs. Jodie Hamilton fell into that category. Widows were often romantically vulnerable, though he was at the moment in no mood to offer services beyond the call of duty. There was, to the best of his knowledge, no panic over medical expenses or school fees. Besides, his wife, Soo-ling, had to be handled with care. She was always suspicious of large tips.

As the passengers disembarked, Krishna envied the guides assigned to one-day tours. They would be rid of blue-rinsed hair and gross, unbecoming buttocks by evening, whereas he had to mouth tall tales, potted histories and facile flatteries for the next seven days.

He held up his placard with resignation as he ticked off mentally the elements in the deluxe programme. A funicular ride to the top of Penang Hill, viewing rusting cannons at Fort

Cornwallis, visiting the Snake Temple with its dozing pit vipers, feeding the Rhesus monkeys at the Botanical Garden, walking the beach at Batu Ferringhi, inspecting a motley selection of temples and mosques. The whole thing should not last three days. The trick was to spin it out for another four.

After a while, he saw a woman in a cotton frock of a bright floral design taking leave of fellow passengers. She strode majestically towards him, on long, elegant legs. She looked cool and crisp and young in the colourful dress. He then noticed the dazzling blue eyes and the blonde curls cascading upon her shoulders like burnished gold.

"Hi! I'm Jodie Hamilton," the vision said, extending a well-manicured hand. Her voice was soft but deep-throated.

Krishna caught a whiff of expensive perfume. The handclasp was firm and friendly. He flashed a smile in response, displaying a set of strong white teeth.

"Welcome to Penang, Mrs. Hamilton," he said, in English carrying a distinctive Dravidian lilt. "Krishna of Paradise Tours has the honour to be at your service. A car is waiting. If Madam will identify her luggage, I will escort Madam to the hotel."

He noted swiftly that the lady was older than he had at first imagined, for he could now discern an incipient double chin and a certain pleasing maturity in the fullness of the figure. He judged her to be around her mid-thirties.

"Krishna? Isn't that the name of a god in these parts?" Mrs. Hamilton asked, with a warm smile.

"Yes, M'am. Krishna is the Hindu god of fire, lightning, storms, the heavens and the sun, the eighth avatar of Vishnu."

"Well, seven days in paradise escorted by a Hindu god is not to be sneezed at. I'm looking forward to it. But let's drop the formality. Just call me 'Jodie'. We Americans don't go in much for formality."

"That is most pleasing to know. May I suggest a walk around the city after checking in? That way, your bearings will be — how do you say it — better oriented? The streets around here can be confusing. When you are ready, I suggest lunch in the hotel."

"I don't lunch, Krish. But don't forsake your meal break on my account." Mrs. Hamilton's blue eyes sparkled beguilingly as she spoke. "You don't mind my calling you Krish, do you? It sounds more friendly. I'm not being too familiar, am I? I don't want to go against local usage."

"No, not at all. Krish will be most acceptable."

"Good. Now, Krish, don't worry about me food-wise. Forget about hamburgers and sirloin steaks. I'm very adventurous. I'll eat anything. In fact, I'm dying to sample the local fare."

"That is also most heartening to know," Krishna said, mesmerized by the blue eyes and the dulcet tones coming from the soft painted mouth. "As you can see, we are a multi-racial and multi-cultural society. So we have a wide choice in food, ranging from Malay to Indian to Chinese, plus some hybrid dishes known as nyonya food. It will be my pleasure to introduce you to whatever you wish."

"Great. Let's get the luggage and be on our way."

After checking in, Mrs. Hamilton repaired to her room to freshen up. As Krishna waited in the hotel lobby, he could not suppress a ripple of excitement. What luck! He has actually landed an attractive American for a change! He wondered if her adventurousness over food extended to other appetites.

He tried to think of ways of eliciting further information about his charge. But when she rejoined him, he found himself on the receiving end of questions instead.

"I hope you don't mind a lot of silly questions, Krish," Mrs. Hamilton said, diffidently, as they strolled out of the hotel. "It is just that I know so little about this part of the world. The main thing about travelling is to get to know other cultures, isn't it? There seems to be so many different races here that I can't tell exactly who are the natives and who are the transplants. Are you, for example, indigenous to these parts?"

"Not really. I'm a transplant, although this is the only home I know," Krishna replied. "My family are Tamils, from southern India. My grandparents came as indentured labourers, to work as tappers in rubber plantations. My father was born here but my mother came from India upon marriage. She and my father also worked as tappers, although my father is now a foreman. I was born here and was lucky enough to get sufficient schooling to become a tourist guide. That's progress, I suppose."

"Good for you! And what is a tapper?"

"Well, a tapper goes out early in the morning to slice the barks of rubber trees. That causes a milky fluid called latex to ooze out. The latex drips into small cups place at the bottom of each cutting. At the end of the day the latex is collected for processing. I can show you tomorrow."

"I would love that. Your family is now settled here for good?"

"Well, yes and no. My grandparents are dead. But I think my parents still feel more Indian than Malaysian. They observe Indian festivals and stick pretty much to old habits and customs. They visit India whenever they have enough money. I think they would rather go back if they could make a decent living there.

"But not me. This is the only home I know, although I don't feel I quite belong. When I was in school, this country was ruled by the British. Now it is independent, and it is ruled by the Malays. Either way, I'm a second-class citizen. The trouble is that India doesn't mean much to me either. I've never been there and I've no desire to go.

"I can't speak Tamil at all well, let alone read and write it. I was taught only Malay and English at school. Some call that cultural imperialism. But whatever it is called, there's no denying people like me are getting messed up culturally. Marriages across racial and religious lines make matters worse. To be honest, I am only Indian in my appearance and in my choice of food."

"Oh, how sad!" Mrs. Hamilton said, with undisguised sympathy. "Let us at least honour that part of your heritage by having an Indian meal this evening. But I want the real McCoy, not stuff served up in fancy restaurants for tourists."

"Indian food can be very hot."

"I'm used to that. I've had plenty of Mexican food in Texas and some of that's pretty darn hot."

"Ah, but not as hot as vindaloo. People say vindaloo is so hot that if you fed it to a corpse it would sit up!"

"That I've got to try!"

That evening Krishna took Mrs. Hamilton to a traditional Indian restaurant. It was an unpretentious place, consisting of a large whitewashed hall resonating with lilting tones. Dark-faced customers shared benches before long wooden tables. Cuttings of banana leaves served as plates. The advent of a blonde woman brought a momentary hush to the room. Then the babble resumed.

Waiters in bare feet circulated with large earthen pots filled with Madras and vindaloo curries, tandoori chicken, grilled tiger prawns the size of lobsters, bhendi bhaji, boiled rice and Indian pancakes served with a lentils gravy. Portions were ladled onto the banana leaves on request.

"No eating utensils here, dear lady. You'll have to eat with your hand," Krishna explained. "You make your food into a small ball and pop it into your mouth. But use only your right hand. The left is considered unclean. When you have finished, there are wash basins in the back."

"Why is the left hand unclean?"

"Because it is used for other purposes."

A puzzled look crossed Mrs. Hamilton's face. Then she caught the meaning. "Right! I get it! Gosh, one learns something new everyday. A left-handed person must be in trouble in this place!"

Krishna also introduced Mrs. Hamilton to toddy, the potent fermented palm alcohol popular among Indians. She took to it readily and by the end of the evening they were both in a merry mood.

"You've done us proud, Krish," Mrs. Hamilton said. "If tonight is anything to go by, we're going to have a fabulous time together."

When Krishna got home, Soo-ling said: "You're late and you've been drinking. Don't tell me you've been with your cronies again."

"No, lah," Krishna replied, with a slur in his voice. "It's work, lah. An American widow on that damn deluxe tour. I'm stuck with her all week."

"If she keeps you out this late, I hope she's a big tipper. We're running tight again and I don't want to have to go to my father."

"What! Again?'

In order to deflect him, Soo-ling said: "Look at your shirt, lah! You've got curry on it! That's devilish to clean, man. Can't you be more careful?"

The toddy had mellowed Krishna to such an extent that he soon fell asleep, oblivious to both the family's shaky finances and his wife's admonitions.

The next morning, he showed Mrs. Hamilton a rubber plantation. It surprised him that she should find pleasure in walking around in the dank, dark shade of rubber trees, watching the slow trickle of white latex into tin receptacles. Their drinking the previous night had broken the ice so the walk in the rubber plantation proved quite companionable.

After the walk Krishna took her on the funicular to Penang Hill, the location of one of the earliest colonial hill stations in the country. During the ride, Mrs. Hamilton asked: "Are you married, Krish? Do you have a family of your own?"

"Afraid not."

"I'm surprised. Some smart gal ought to have hog-tied a handsome fella like you before now," Mrs. Hamilton said, in an exaggerated Texas drawl.

"Smart girls like men with money, not tour guides. I can barely support myself, let alone a family. I wanted to marry a Chinese girl once. But our parents objected. The one thing Indian and Chinese parents have in common is to want to arrange their children's marriages! We couldn't get our way. But that's life."

"I'm sorry to hear that! Do you still see the girl?"

"No, she's now married, with two children."

"Oh, how sad!" Mrs. Hamilton placed a hand on Krishna's arm in an expression of sympathy. "I know how it feels to lose someone. I lost Marty — that's Mr. Hamilton — three years ago and I miss him still. We had a few good years together, so I can't really complain. In one of Hemingway's war stories the girl only had four days."

"I've seen that movie! It was about a war in Spain, wasn't it? Didn't Ingrid Bergman play in it? It had such a sad ending."

"Yes, most great love stories seem to have sad endings. It's one of my favourites nonetheless."

They got off the funicular to stroll past the elegant bungalows dotting the hill. Then they walked along lush paths to catch the spectacular vistas of Georgetown and the rest of the island.

On the way back to the funicular, Krishna asked: "What business was Mr. Hamilton in?"

"Oil. Poor Marty! He never had a choice. His grandfather, Martin T. Hamilton, struck oil. By the time he came along his whole life had been mapped out for him. He just became Martin T. Hamilton the Third. He had to suppress his natural, unconventional streak. I think he would rather have been a guitar player or a crop duster. He was that kind of person."

"How strange! I always thought only the poor had no choice."

"Yes, I used to think the same. When Marty died, he left me a forty-room mansion and thirty-five million dollars. Now I'm surrounded by problems. Lawyers, accountants, investment consultants and tax collectors. They drive me crazy. I'm never sure whether people like me or only my money. Rattling around a forty-room mansion by oneself is not much fun either."

"I'm sure plenty of people like you for yourself. You are a very charming lady."

"That's real sweet of you, Krish. But I would give up all I own just to have Marty back again."

"You must care for him a great deal."

"Yes. When we got married, his relatives were against it. They thought I was just after his money. He belonged to the cream of Texas society and I was just a New York showgirl."

"Did Mr. Hamilton meet a tragic end?"

"Tragic? Hell, no! He found the best way to go. He died making love to me. I always told him he worked too hard, both at the office and at home, if you know what I mean. Heck, I don't know why I'm telling you all this. We're practically strangers."

"Ah, some things can only be told to strangers. Isn't that one of the reasons people travel, to unburden themselves to people they need never see again?"

"I didn't realize you are a philosopher, Krish."

They spent the rest of the day inspecting religious monuments and that evening, back in his own home, Krishna tossed in bed trying to visualize what possessing thirty-five million American dollars meant. But he failed. He eventually fell asleep dreaming of what it might be like to expire in Mrs. Hamilton's embrace.

The next day began with a visit to the Botanical Garden, during the course of which Krishna explained that a trip to Batu Ferringhi had been scheduled for the late afternoon.

"There are miles of beach along the northern part of the island," Krishna said. "The only people there are a few fishing families and occasional visitors to the holiday bungalows. The bungalows are owned by business tycoons but they seldom use them. Such a waste. If I owned one I would be there everyday. There's good swimming. The sand is coarse but the water is warm and clear."

"That sounds great," Mrs. Hamilton said. "I'll buy that."

Later that day Mrs. Hamilton presented herself in a wide-brimmed straw hat, dark glasses, a loose-fitting Hawaiian dress and a pair of leather sandals. A large tote bag hung from one shoulder. Her attire lent her an air of casual sophistication, like that of a movie actress at play.

Upon arrival, Krishna parked the car and pointed to an outcrop of granite jutting onto the beach. "The name of the beach is derived from that pile of rocks," he explained. "In the days of sailing ships,

Portuguese and Dutch sailors used to land here for fresh water. Thus the place became known as Batu Ferringhi or Foreigner's Rock."

"The beach looks marvellous," Mrs. Hamilton said, breathing in the clean sea air. "Shall we walk a while before we take to the water?"

"As you wish," Krishna replied. "You're the paying guest."

As they strolled along the beach fringed with palms, casuarinas and other tropical growths, a gentle breeze brought the distant scent of frangipani. Tiny sand crabs scurried out of their way. Except for a few children splashing in the water, they had the beach to themselves.

After a while they found a suitable place to rest and Mrs. Hamilton indicated her readiness for a swim. She removed her Hawaiian dress to reveal a smart two-piece bathing costume, which displayed her buxom figure to advantage. She began applying sun tan lotion to her limbs and body but asked Krishna to help put some on her back.

As Krishna applied the lotion, the plasticity of the smooth, warm flesh electrified him with desire. His hand almost strayed beyond permissible bounds. He suddenly remembered another time at the very same beach when he had been similarly excited while rubbing sun tan lotion on the back of a Chinese girl. That had led to a pregnancy and the near-banishment of both of them from their respective families.

"Done," he said quickly, handing back the lotion.

"Aren't you going to swim with me?" Mrs. Hamilton asked, as she made ready to enter the water.

"That is not allowed when I'm on duty. I have to watch your possessions and act as lifeguard in case of difficulties."

"There won't be difficulties. I'm a strong swimmer," Mrs. Hamilton said, as she ran towards the sea.

As Krishna watched Mrs. Hamilton swimming with a strong crawl, he felt stirred again by desire. The palm of his hand still tingled from the contact with her flesh. He could sense a physical hunger in her and he felt an overwhelming urge to possess her.

After half an hour, Mrs. Hamilton came out of the sea with a majestic langour of a goddess. Her near nakedness was almost too much for Krishna to bear.

"The water was super. You should have joined me," Mrs. Hamilton said, pulling a hotel towel out from her tote bag to dry her hair, leaving it tousled and child-like. She then put on her sunglasses and lowered herself onto the sand. As she stretched out, her bosom rose and fell in rhythm with her breathing. The studs of her nipples were outlined clearly beneath her wet costume, while the golden down on her limbs caught the last rays of the retreating sun.

Krishna could think of nothing but ravishing that wet, delectable body. It seemed so ripe, earthy and available. Only the fear of being sacked deterred him from chancing an initiative. Because of the sunglasses, he could not tell whether Mrs. Hamilton was watching him or whether she had her eyes closed. Nevertheless he blatantly devoured every tempting feature of her body with his eyes.

Dusk came with tropical swiftness, aided by a steady gathering of rain clouds. After what seemed an interminable silence, Mrs. Hamilton said: "This is truly paradise. Warm water and clean air, the sense of emptiness and serenity. Everything here is so unspoilt and simple that life itself appears simple. I feel restored, as if I have caught a glimpse of eternity itself. I could come back here again and again."

That sudden interruption of Krishna's private fantasies caused a blind, mindless rage to explode in him. All the secret resentments he had harboured against the moneyed complacencies of foreign tourists flared in him. Who did they think they were, coming into his world and flaunting their wealth and their bodies, compelling him to do their bidding? The resentments were all the more acute because he knew he could be bought.

"You should leave and never come back," he said, abruptly.

The harshness in his tone of voice caused Mrs. Hamilton to prop herself up on one elbow and to remove her sunglasses. "Why?" she asked, baffled and sounding hurt.

"We in the East are hospitable by nature. But when outsiders come they alter what we have and nothing is the same again. We turn ourselves inside out for the tourist dollar and begin missing what we never wanted before. The government has just given permission for a luxury hotel to be built on this very spot.

"Just imagine this place ten or fifteen years from now. The whole beach will be jammed with holiday makers on package tours. Fisherfolk and farmers will be turned into waiters and chambermaids, quarrelling over the division of their tips. Tour buses will jam the roads and sewage will pollute the sea. I will have to watch such things happening. I have no forty-room mansion in Dallas to escape to."

"Oh, I'm sorry, Krish!" Mrs. Hamilton said. "I haven't thought of things that way. I've been so insensitive." She gazed deeply into Krishna's eyes and lifted a comforting hand to touch his cheek.

And before anyone knew it, they were in each other's arms and the last four days of the deluxe tour were passed largely in Mrs. Hamilton's luxurious hotel room.

Krishna conquered Mrs. Hamilton as he had done in his most intimate dreams. His hands, both clean and unclean, searched out her sweet mysteries. She was different from the others, he told himself, through a haze of passion. To her he could give something of himself. During moments of exhaustion he wondered fleetingly whether he might be falling in love. But another part of him speculated upon what it might be like to drive around Dallas in one of those red, convertible Thunderbirds he had seen in glossy magazines.

When time came for them to part, Krishna said: "I didn't mean what I said about not wanting you to come back. I shall always be here, thinking of you, longing for you."

"Thanks for everything," Mrs. Hamilton said. "But I think you are right about never coming back. Things can never be the same again, can they? Hemingway's Maria had four days of love. So have I. I shouldn't be greedy. Goodbye, my dear Hindu god, and look after yourself."

As she extended her hand in farewell, she pressed something into Krishna's hand.

Krishna drove out to the beach at Foreigner's Rock after seeing Mrs. Hamilton off. He sat down on the warm sand and slowly unfolded the piece of paper that had been pressed into his hand. It was a cheque for five thousand American dollars.

What did it mean, Krishna asked himself, as he stared at it. Why had he been given a cheque for something which was beyond any price? Had it meant nothing more to her than just another service rendered? And what was the use of such a cheque anyway? It wouldn't help the family finances. He would never be able to explain to Soo-ling why an American widow should tip him so generously.

The English Secretary

As Mr. Fu waited for his guests in the lounge of the Victoria Cricket Club, he wondered if he had really — in the parlance of his English secretary — "arrived." Pip had a way of whizzing words past him so that it took a while to capture their undertones. He pondered whether Pip was just trying to justify his decision to leave.

Over the last seven years Mr. Fu had become so dependent upon that young Englishman that his tendering of notice came as a shock.

"You see, Sir, politicians back home are bungling the future of this place," Pip explained, with that bemused candour, which enlivened his steel-grey eyes. "They're very good at making others pay for their mistakes and one day people here will undoubtedly have to pay. So it's best that I move on before I get numbered among the bunglers. Besides, you don't need me any more. You've arrived.'

Mr. Fu wasn't sure what was being bungled or what secret intelligence Pip possessed. Though rumours of shady dealings over Hong Kong had been circulating for years, the lease on the New Territories still had a decade and a half to run. So far as he was concerned, politicians could play whatever games they liked so long as they left him alone to make money, for only money could buy the ultimate freedom to do as one chose.

What he could not figure out, however, was why a young man of intelligence should have failed to seize upon that fundamental truth. Pip seemed contented with his salary and indifferent to business opportunities all around him. Regardless of what politicians might be up to, why not exploit the greatest wealth-creating city in the world?

The English were a curious race, he reflected. Until Pip shed light on them, they were a complete mystery. Their concepts, like the rule of law and the presumption of innocence, were brilliant. The notion that companies could assume legal identities separate from their operators was ingenious. Dicey dealings behind corporate veils, holding companies in tax havens, hot money flowing through Montserrat, Anguilla, the Turks and Caicos and other seldom mentioned places. What marvellous opportunities for enrichment! Yet, after setting them in place, the English seemed to prefer watching birds, digging up gardens or attending to the comfort of cats and dogs!

The Number One Boy in the lounge moved forward smartly to offer an aperitif but Mr. Fu waved him away with a smile. He smiled altogether too readily. When he did so, friendly wrinkles would spread outwards from the corners of his soft brown eyes and downwards from the sides of his nostrils, to wreath his wide, almost simian mouth with bonhomie.

The propensity to smile was a habit developed since boyhood. It was a sort of defensive mechanism to obscure his deficient English, his lack of social polish and, most of all, his diminutive build. How could anyone project a commanding presence standing at less than five-foot-one?

Nevertheless nature had compensated him with a nose for business and a determination to succeed. Those qualities had enabled him to turn an insignificant electrician's shop inherited from his father at the age of seventeen into one of Hong Kong's real-estate giants.

His rise had been steady, his method ludicrously simple. In the course of rewiring dilapidated tenements or repairing electrical faults, it occurred to him some must be ripe for redevelopment. When he noticed an unusual number of unoccupied sub-divisions in a building, he suspected redevelopment must be afoot.

So, backing his hunch, he would scrape together enough to acquire a nook or a cubicle, in order to frustrate demolition until someone paid his price. One such successful gamble earned him more than two years of installing air-conditioning units or rewiring apartments. When such successes multiplied, he began dealing in real estate himself. Thereafter it was just a matter of timely speculations during the colony's successive property booms.

But acquiring wealth was one thing, gaining social acceptability was another. One could not buy the latter as one might a skyscraper or a shopping mall. The old money crowd still looked down their noses at him and he recalled with barely suppressed bitterness being black-balled twice by the Membership Committee of the Victoria Cricket Club.

Mr. Fu had no attachment to the outlandish game, which ruled the passions of the club's mainly expatriate members. Moreover, he loathed its somnolent air, its red velvet curtains, its arcane traditions and its attachments to long-buried players. It was only the notion of people without a fraction of his wealth passing judgment on him that perversely steeled his resolve to be admitted. Generous contributions to certain quarters eventually secured admission.

After attaining membership, his only interest centred upon the club's spacious grounds. The clubhouse was an antiquated building, filled with useless columns Pip had once described as "mock Corinthian, designed for Victorian little Englanders."

He had no idea what that meant but he knew fortunes could be had through better utilization of a prime site at the heart of the city. He visualized the oval being tastefully fringed with stands and a tower block to house a redesigned clubhouse with indoor recreational facilities. That would still leave room for two other office blocks for letting. Rental income would secure the finances of the club for decades to come. He would, of course, make a few dollars too if granted the right to develop the project. So he put his ideas to the Executive Committee, only to have them rejected out of hand by a lot of old fogies.

But barely three years later, the club appointed a European consortium to redevelop facilities along the lines he had originally envisaged. It was during such moments that an unreasoning xenophobic malice welled up in him. It made him want to live long enough to see the advent of the Communists, who might expropriate that prime site for a People's Memorial Park to the forgotten martyrs of colonial oppression!

Mr. Fu's agitation was soothed by the arrival of his Canadian guests, escorted by Pip. Mr. Fu beamed his wrinkled smile and shook hands warmly. The guests were prospective partners for a Vancouver joint venture. Although he outranked them in wealth, he nevertheless felt an awkwardness speaking up to those towering a head above him.

He led the procession to the club's Gladstone Room, where Pip had arranged a quiet corner table. Once seated, however, he felt more in command. If he got waylaid by an English word or phrase, Pip could always be counted on to come to the rescue.

Since Pip came into his life, he had lost his fear of the glittering array of glasses and eating utensils confronting him in the Gladstone Room. Nor was he any longer intimidated by the unintelligible wine lists. Pip had simplified everything down to No. 17 for white and No. 43 for red. Pip had taught him to simulate wine-tasting and so long as he remembered whether it was No. 17 or No. 43 he was referring to, he could recite a remark or two about vintage, bouquet or mellowness.

The meal went swimmingly and the serious business of catering for Vancouver's demand for luxury apartments was left for the office the following day.

When Mr. Fu got home, he could not help wondering what he would ever do without Pip. Those charitable operatic evenings he was obliged to attend would revert to absolute nightmares. He couldn't tell the difference between Puccini, Wagner or anybody else. It all sounded like so much caterwauling. Worse still was the requirement to be stuffed in an evening suit like a tailor's dummy.

Pip made such evenings less intolerable by providing a synopsis to explain each story. He also supplied apt remarks to drop during intervals. They might just be "It's not exactly La Scala." or "His room in Briennerstrasse must have been something!"

Mr. Fu had not the slightest notion what the remarks meant. But they seemed to produce an awed effect.

Mr. Fu first encountered Pip when he went to London to acquire a commercial complex in the City of London and to install his youngest child, Melody, at Roedean. After completing both missions, he decided to see the sights in London.

Mr. Hanson, his lead banker, offered the services of his favourite nephew. "You'll find him extremely likeable and knowledgeable," Mr. Hanson said. "He was educated at Winchester and Oxford and belongs to a very distinguished family. But hasn't quite settled down, you know. I got him started at a stockbroker's but he found that distasteful. Then I secured him a position in one of our branches. But he got too chummy with the manager's wife. Pity. He seems to attract women like flies."

Because of his unfamiliarity with London and because the young man sounded intriguing, Mr. Fu accepted, and that was how he met Pip.

Actually, the nephew's name was not Pip at all. It was Richard Remmington-Rowe. But Mr. Fu's command of English was such that it came out as "Litchit Lemingdon-Low". The young man spotted the impediment at once and suggested "Pip", a nickname formerly bestowed by his nanny. The young man's graciousness did not pass unnoticed.

Pip impressed Mr. Fu with other qualities as well. He had a natural hauteur and cultivation, which Mr. Fu envied. When passing the venerable portals of Coutts, Pip observed: "This is the place to put your money if you want to rub accounts with the Queen." Mr. Fu duly took note and opened an account shortly thereafter.

Apart from the usual London sights, Pip also introduced Mr. Fu to those remarkable little shops along Jermyn Street, studded with plaques testifying to a variety of royal patronages. Under Pip's guidance he ordered tailor-made pajamas with monograms, a silver cigar-cutter engraved with his name, a shaving brush and mug, bath salts and a host of other items he had hitherto never felt any need for. He enjoyed himself enormously, however, for up to that point consumption had consisted largely of signing cheques for the extravagances of his wife and children.

After a couple of days, Pip introduced Mr. Fu to an institution favoured by English dowagers — afternoon tea at Fortnum & Mason. Mr. Fu was much amused and it suddenly occurred to him that Pip might be just the man to throw light on that indolent game played at the Victoria Cricket Club.

It transpired Pip was a cricketer of considerable standing and was a member of one of the leading British clubs. Mr. Fu listened carefully to the expositions about googlies and innings and the nine ways of putting out a batsman. But what touched him was Pip's explanation of the mock cremation of English cricket following the Australian victory in 1882 and the subsequent reference to the return of the ashes. When Pip took him to Lord's, the resting place of the mythical ashes, he appreciated for the first time that the English, like the Chinese, delighted in eccentricities.

By the end of the week, Mr. Fu was so taken by Pip that he asked Mr. Hanson if his nephew might consider a job in Hong Kong.

"I'm not sure," Mr. Hanson answered. "In another age he would be a gentleman of leisure. But primogeniture and death duties have put paid to that. Heading for the colonies used to be an alternative but nowadays all that's left is Hong Kong."

"Plentee money in Hong Kong still," Mr. Fu said. "I can use good man to do diss and dat."

"Well, I'll sound him out, if you think the way Richard attracts women is not a problem."

Mr. Fu thought fleeting of his wife, safely thirty years Pip's senior. Of his two daughters, the elder was married and well on the way to producing a third child. As for Melody, she was securely cooling the fevers of puberty in the draughty dormitories of Roedean. There were, of course, the three Filipino maids. But liaisons among employees were none of his business. Thus reassured, he said: "Please let me know what he dinks."

Within three months Pip arrived in Hong Kong. Since Mr. Fu's children had homes of their own or had migrated and Melody was in boarding school, it was decided that Pip should stay at the under-utilized Fu mansion. Mr. Fu hoped that Pip might provide company during his morning dips in the pool. Besides, his wife's English, more shaky than his own, could do with help.

At the corporate headquarters, Pip was assigned an office next to Mr. Fu's. He had no formal title, however, so he gradually got referred to as "the English secretary". His presence caused quite a stir at first, for no one knew how to handle a foreigner in a Chinese enterprise. Apart from the hurdles of language, there was also apprehension over his uncertain relationship with the boss.

But Pip gradually won everybody over with his gentlemanliness and charm. When not attending to mysterious tasks assigned by Mr. Fu, he spent his time reading books on jade, snuff bottles, herbal medicine, Taoist philosophy, Chinese history and the like. The young secretaries and female clerks soon started eyeing him with those dreamy looks usually reserved for popular crooners and unattainable screen idols. It was little different around the home. The Filipino maids fell over themselves to attend to his creature comforts.

Pip quickly adjusted to Chinese customs. He stuck gallantly to chopsticks during meals and each morning greeted Mr. and Mrs. Fu deferentially, in a manner appropriate for a member of a younger generation. In no time Mrs. Fu began treating him like a son.

It was during Pip's second summer in Hong Kong that he met Melody. She had gone on a grand tour of European cities the previous summer. She was a pretty, petite girl of sixteen and might have appeared prettier if she had exchanged her over-sized spectacles for contact lenses and softened her serious demeanour by smiling as readily as her father.

Mr. Fu took great pride in Melody. "She was top of klass," he said, upon introducing Melody to Pip. He had expected Pip to offer congratulations. Instead Pip said: "I wouldn't do that again, if I were you. It's bad form to appear too keen."

After his initial shock, Mr. Fu recalled the Chinese adage about over-educated daughters ending up as old maids. How astute Pip was! What Melody needed were not academic distinctions or skills to earn a living but the qualities to attract a good husband! Her bent towards a doctorate in physics or organic chemistry or some such heady subject had to be deflected!

In due course Mr. Fu sought Pip's counsel.

"Let her finish at Roedean. Then send her for detoxification in a Swiss finishing school," Pip suggested. "After that, she should be over her Madam Curie phase. University will do no great harm if she sticks to something amusing."

Mr. Fu reflected on the passage of the years as he prepared for bed. His wife, who seldom accompanied him on business dinners with foreigners, was already fast asleep.

Thanks to Pip, Melody ended finishing school cured of further thoughts of scientific glory. She was now at the point of leaving university, where she had involved herself in dramatic productions and studying the romantic poets. A safe preparation for life, Mr. Fu concluded, and one unlikely to scare off the prospective husbands his wife was sniffing out.

The next morning Mr. Fu told his wife of Pip's impending departure. Mrs. Fu accepted in poor grace the loss of a young man who had taught her so many clever things to impress society ladies. They presented him with a platinum Constantin watch as a parting gift.

For weeks following Pip's departure Mr. Fu experienced a strange sense of disquiet, as if a centre of balance in his life could no longer be located. Soon thereafter, on his sixty-fifth birthday, he received a present from Pip in the form of a green jade pendant carved in the form of a Chinese "peach of longevity."

He felt immensely touched. But as he thought about the young man who had schooled him in so many of the modish conventions of the West, he wondered if something of the East might have rubbed off on Pip in return, things that business types like himself were progressively forgetting. He recalled an ancient sage counselling against wise men acquiring too much wealth, lest it harmed their ideals. Was that a truth that Pip had taken on board? Was that what frightened him into abandoning Hong Kong? Was he seeking a freedom different from that provided by wealth?

A glimmer of understanding slowly dawned upon Mr. Fu and it filled him with a wistful sadness.

"The English Secretary" has been broadcast by the British Broadcasting Corporation on Radio 4 in Britain, by Radio Netherlands in Holland and by Radio Belgium in Belgium.

Hand of Innocence

"Help yourself," the headman said, matter-of-factly, as he indicated an open-sided thatched shed at the far edge of the half-empty village. His face, gaunt and wrinkled, seemed devoid of emotion and his eyes suggested he had seen more than he wanted.

Nhoung showed his appreciation in the traditional way, by placing his palms together in front of his broad, brown face. His long, black hair, gathered into a ponytail, and his frazzled moustache lent him a certain bohemian air. He took his leave of the headman and made his way dispiritedly in the direction indicated, along the earthen track meandering around the scattered huts of the village.

He felt wrung out. He had forgotten how sapping the tropical heat could be before the monsoons came. He had endured it for days, travelling in unreliable transport and across dangerous terrain, in order to reach this out-of-the-way Cambodian village near the border with Thailand

The distance between this primitive, uninviting place, with its lingering odour of death, and Paris, with its pious building and orderly boulevards, seemed like a journey from one universe to another. Now that he had reached it he was not sure what he wanted to find.

A few scrawny children with faces evocative of Oxfam posters peered at him shyly from the doorways of flimsy huts. He allowed his generous mouth to break into a smile but the children responded by withdrawing a little into the huts. No doubt his sweaty denim shirt with its rolled up sleeves and his soiled Levi jeans marked him as an outsider and they had cause to be wary. He felt an instinctive need to reach them, to tell them that he was not there to cause harm but only to rediscover his purpose, his family and his country.

But he could not find the words. His long exile in France, while sparing him the starvations and butcheries besetting his nation, also effectively turned him into a stranger without shared experiences.

His departure from home had been quite innocent. It happened a long time ago. He wanted to become a painter. Ever since boyhood he had found delight in sketching his sisters practising court dances and capturing on paper the lichen covered temples of Angkor Wat and Angkor Thom. When his French teachers, discovering his interest, introduced him to the works of Renoir, Monet, Utrillo, Dufy, Bonnard, Vulliard, Daumier and countless others, he became hopelessly hooked.

It seemed that studying in Paris, following in the footsteps of those masters, could be nothing short of heaven. So he badgered his father, a wealthy timber merchant, to dispatch him to the City of Light.

His father, however, had different ideas. Cambodia needed doctors, engineers and irrigation experts rather than painters, his father declared. Pictures could neither ease hunger nor cure diseases. He wanted his son to go into a profession.

But Nhoung was adamant. Being the eldest of three sons, after two girls, and the apple of both his mother's and his grandmother's eye, his unhappiness over his father's refusal soon caused the womenfolk to bring more subtle persuasions into play. At the age of seventeen he was granted his wish. His mother hung a gold chain around his neck attached to a small jade image of Buddha to protect him from evil and to remind him to recite the Sutras. He was then shipped off tearfully to France.

Paris went to his head. He installed himself in one of those charming studio apartments with sagging floors and balustraded windows and threw himself into his art. Forms and colours simply exploded from his brushes and that was all he lived for.

So absorbed was he with his studies and paintings that he paid no attention to the subtle shifts in military and political alignments touched upon in letters from home. In any event he had a loathing for politics, with its ready expediencies and its back-room deals, and did not share his father's royalist sympathies.

He began to feel uneasy only when the phony neutrality prevailing at the time of his departure erupted into a complex internecine conflict, with some Cambodians choosing to serve in the United States Special Forces and others siding with the Viet Cong. Still others played all sides and grew rich in the process. When the Americans eventually withdrew from Indochina, the Khmer Rouge began their march to power.

At first they did not appeared so awesome. The peasants supported them. Indeed, some idealistic compatriots headed swiftly home to aid in the rebirth and reconstruction of the nation. Only his father remained pessimistic. But he discounted that as the view of someone who had lived most of his life in a mummified French colonial protectorate, tied to the ways of the old regime.

Suddenly word came from his father, ordering him to remain in France until further notice. His father told him he was evacuating the entire family to Thailand. That would be a massive undertaking because the immediate family was made up of thirty-three mouths, including his grandmother, his parents, his sisters and brothers, their husbands and wives, and their numerous children.

He thought the move too drastic. So far as he was aware, the Khmer Rouge were only attempting to even out the disparities between the cities and the countryside by abolishing the use of money and by ordering the evacuation of the urban areas. There might be the odd unpleasantness but Cambodians were by and large Buddhists, for whom the taking of life was a sin. Moreover,

Prince Sihanouk was still Head of State. So he persuaded himself that the excesses of other revolutions were unlikely to occur.

But that was the last he heard from his family. All attempts to make contact or to secure information failed. The Khmer Rouge had apparently made total secrecy the basis of their administration.

As Nhoung trudged along the village path he reflected on how wrong he had been. The Khmer Rouge, under Pol Pot, turned out to be monsters. They wanted to take the nation back to what they called "Year Zero", when it was supposed to be ethnically pure and uncontaminated by religion, imperialist ideas and the corruption of urban ways. To achieve that they started slaughtering racial and religious minorities, monks, political opponents and even those within their own ranks who voiced dissent. Idealists and patriots who had returned from abroad met similar fates.

Nhoung noticed some villagers working in the fields beyond the huts. He would never be at one with them again, he thought. While they were toiling in the tropical heat he was strolling in the Luxembourg Garden; while they were being starved and tortured, he was mouthing inanities about art in Left Bank cafes; and while they were watching their friends and loved ones led to the killing fields, he was drowning his pride with pernod because his paintings had failed to dazzle the world.

There was now supposed to be peace, brokered by the United Nations. But peace was not simply the absence of full-scale war. How could there be peace when the Khmer Rouge still lurked in the jungles, when the country was carved up among armed factions, when gunfire resounded during the night to leave bullet-riddled bodies the following morning and when innocent people were being blown apart every day by mines planted by the Americans, by the Vietnamese, by Sihanoukists, by Lon Nol sympathizers, by the Khmer Rouge and by Hun Sen supporters?

No one knew how many mines there were or where they had been buried. The best guesses ran into millions. His country had become the ultimate dream for arms suppliers. It offered daily proof of the cost-effectiveness of their killing machines!

He would have gladly abandoned his accursed land to its self-seeking politicians and generals if distant relatives in Bangkok had not passed on rumours about his immediate family. Apparently someone had heard from someone else who had seen his parents at this particular village during their flight from Phnom Penh. The fact that none of his family had reached Thailand was certain. Given the years of silence, he had long suspected the worst. It was now a matter of facing up to the truth.

After the Vietnamese had overthrown the Khmer Rouge, it was revealed that most of the inhabitants of the village and others who had fled there had perished from starvation, disease or executions. If such terrible fates had befallen his family, he had at least to locate their remains and arrange decent burials. The village headman told him all remains recovered from mass graves, minus those already identified and buried, were located at the open-sided shed at the edge of the village.

Nhoung arrived at last at the shed. There before him, on a wooden platform, was a huge pyramid of bleached, grimacing skulls, some partially smashed and others still wearing the rotting blindfolds of execution. The dark apertures which once provided for the human senses still seemed to retain lingering echoes of terminal traumas. Next to the pyramid of skulls was a great heap of other remains — rib cages, spinal columns, hip bones, femurs, ulnas and the rest.

Nhoung collapsed upon his knees and his body heaved with unchecked tears. He suddenly saw the ghastly form and substance of the killing fields, hitherto known only in the abstract. He thought he had gone beyond anger, beyond pain, beyond grief. But he was wrong. A great, nameless anguish seized his heart.

How many must have suffered to leave such monuments to madness! How could he possibly identify his family members from such jumbled remains? He remembered his grandmother had two gold teeth. He laughed bitterly at that wayward thought. To imagine that any skull could have retained two gold teeth for so long was completely idiotic!

Picasso had painted Guernica to express his outrage at what the Fascists had done in Spain. But the horrors of Guernica had been inflicted from the air, at a distance, impersonally, almost clinically. What lay before him spoke of atrocities done at close quarters, in cold blood, with even demonic glee. How could anyone find the appropriate symbols and colours to express carnage on such a scale?

He wanted to bury each of the dead before him but knew it would be impossible. There was no telling which bones belonged with which skull. He picked from the pile of bones a tiny set of ulna and radius, with all the fingers still attached. It had been a child's. It could easily have belonged to one of his nephews or nieces.

He held the bleached relic and gently rubbed away some mud clinging to the finger bones. After a while, he brushed the tear stains from his face and went looking for the headman. When he had found him, he asked: "Where might I bury my family?"

"You have identified them?" the headman asked, with the merest hint of surprise in his voice.

"No," Nhoung replied, holding up the bone. "But I have found the hand of an innocent child. What better to represent what I and our entire nation have lost. Where can I bury it?"

"Anywhere you like beyond the village. Perhaps on the edge of the jungle. Be careful, however, not to wander too far, lest you add your own bones to the pile. There are mines out there."

Nhoung borrowed a hoe from the headman and made his way to the edge of the jungle. He dug a deep hole so that the relic might rest without risk of being disturbed. After he had placed it into the hole, he unclasped the jade Buddha from the gold chain around his neck and deposited it within the bony web of fingers. He then buried them and marked the site with a pile of rocks so that he could find it should he ever venture that way again.

He rested himself upon the stem of the hoe, sweating and dirty but with a sense of having discharged an obligation. What now? Should he abandon Cambodia to its self-inflicted chaos, as most of the world had already done, and to watch from a safe distance its steady decline into anarchy and atavism? Or should he attempt to salvage what he could from the wreckage? But that could a painter of no consequence achieve? What difference would one man make?

He thought of the mines recklessly scattered everywhere. So long as they existed, there would be continuing tragedies and fresh excuses for apportioning blame. That was probably why the warring factions remained indifferent to clearing them.

There was a small band of dedicated people, however, many of them foreigners, who had taken it upon themselves to destroy the mines, to stop innocent civilians and children being maimed or killed. He had met some of them during his journey and they had told him of the delicate and hazardous nature of their work.

Well, he could do worse than to join them. He too could learn to brush away the earth harbouring those deadly devices. It would provide work enough for a lifetime. The instruments previously employed to paint the tinctures of skin and flowers onto canvas could just as easily be used to serve a more immediately humane purpose. Perhaps his poor father had been wrong after all in thinking that Cambodia had no need for painters.

Aftershock

It had been ten days since the funeral, and Hannah still could not get used to the notion of widowhood. It was most inconsiderate of Chai to get run over by a bus, she thought, for it was a death without style. It was the kind of death meant for doddering old ladies with failing eyesight and not for a man in the prime of life. It then crossed her mind it might be stretching a point to describe a man of forty-nine with three grown-up children as being in his prime.

She sat at Chai's desk at the bank and looked at the framed photograph which she was about to put into the cardboard box, along with the marble desk set given by the children as a birthday present, the Rotary Club paraphernalia and the rest of his things. It had been kind of Mike Sullivan, the Regional Vice President, to leave Chai's office untouched until she could clear away his belongings.

As she continued with that disagreeable task, she concluded that the photograph looked good, with Chai sitting beside her and the twins and Sharon arraigned behind them. The boys appeared bright and alert and Sharon was a spitting image of herself. There was the same haughty bearing and the same seductive eyes. But then she remembered that they had posed for that more than five years ago, when the boys had returned for their summer holidays and had started that debate as to whether their sister was old enough to go off to boarding school.

As she began sifting through the contents of the drawers, she noted that standard office aids were very much in evidence — a box of Kleenex tissues, bottles of aspirin and antacid pills, business cards, a volume of airline schedules, a few scribbled reminders, some office files, and the usual clutter of paper clips, rubber bands and marking pens.

The more personal items consisted of an address book recording the addresses, telephone numbers, birthdays and anniversaries of close relatives and friends, two letters from the children which Chai had promised to deal with, some postcards from friends and one from a cousin in Australia, several credit card chits, a collection of old receipts, ten copies of a passport photograph, some tourist brochures about Japan where they had intended spending their next vacation, and other oddments. What a pathetic collection to sum up a life, she thought.

Chai's accident was probably more of a disaster for her than for him, Hannah reflected ruefully, as her brow puckered automatically into frown lines. That had become habitual in recent years, whenever she became vexed. Her thin lips, which constituted the most unflattering aspect of her face, compressed themselves petulantly. It was all so aggravating! How could he leave her in the lurch in such a ridiculous manner, just when she had to cope with the trauma of growing old? Death was neat and tidy by comparison.

It was not that Chai would have been much help emotionally in easing her into old age. Or in any other way, apart from the purely financial. He was an unemotional and practical man, unimaginative to a degree in interpersonal relationships. Whatever reserve of warmth and human understanding seemed earmarked for the children and his immediate subordinates. She did not seem to figure anywhere.

Once, when she had complained about his lack of concern for her, he had replied: "That is not true. You know I care for you, so what is the point of trying to demonstrate something you already know? The children are different. They are not certain how much I love them, so I have to go out of my way to show them. You are part of me, as vital as my heart or my eyes or my brain. A man does not go around caressing his heart, his eyes and his brain every day and enquiring how they feel. His concern for them is taken as read. Don't you understand?"

She certainly did not, no matter how irrefutable his logic sounded. Thinking it over did not improve her disposition but she did concede that having him around was probably marginally better than not having him at all.

During the last five years, following the departure of the children and his promotion to chief foreign currency dealer, Chai had maintained the logic of his position. Search as she might, she could not find that crushing counter-argument to dispose of his sophistry. That only led her to retreat frequently into sullen silences.

Apart from the children and certain social obligations, they had really quite little to talk about. Their personal interests hardly coincided, so much so that they led virtually separate lives. He had no interest in her charitable works, her *mah-jong* parties or the society gossip she reported. She, for her part, barely understood the intricacies of his work.

Household affairs needed no consultation. Their servants had long reduced them to a settled routine, and Miss Lam, Chai's secretary of more than twenty years, handled the wages of the servants, the chauffeur and the crew members of the yacht and paid the bills for club dues, credit card expenditures, utility charges and rates with something approaching military efficiency.

Hannah wondered rather belatedly whether Chai's bland and matter-of-fact behaviour might also mask his own concerns over growing old. After all, he was in a line of business dominated by the young and the daring. Although his face had remained relatively youthful and his movements agile, those periodic turmoils in the currency markets must be sapping upon his energies. Those nights of being glued to computer screens in the dealing room, with several telephones screaming simultaneously for attention, had ruined his eyesight and had caused the hair around his temples to turn slightly grey. On the other hand, those pressures did not seem to have forestalled a thickening of his waistline. To his credit he never complained about anything and never brought office worries home.

But what had been most noticeable to Hannah had been Chai's diminished sexual appetite. She felt irritated even thinking about those fortnightly couplings, which passed for conjugal love. The lead-up would be as predictable as the opening gambit in a game of chess and so too would be the end game. Once satisfied, Chai would grunt, turn his back on her and sink into deep and untroubled sleep.

The problem was that long after Chai had been lost to sleep, her whole being would remain agitated and unappeased. If he had only taken the trouble to show more tenderness, to hug and kiss her afterwards, or even to fall asleep with his arms around her, those parodies of the sexual act would have been more tolerable. As it was, her own sleep was often fitful and the mornings found her unrefreshed.

Occasionally, while reading in bed to tire herself out, she would stop and watch Chai lying exposed and unguarded in slumber. Sometimes he would talk in his sleep, crying "Okay! Okay!" or something similar. She could imagine him shouting into telephones and barking orders to his staff at the same time, trying to stay ahead of the game. She had heard that foreign currency dealers often got burnt out early and Chai had been at it longer than most. She would then feel a little sorry over the stressful way in which he had to make a living and would be touched by a momentary regret over her tendency to snap at him.

On such occasions she would also recognize him as the generous, hard-working and uncomplaining husband he was. But, alas, how increasingly unexciting he had become! Their marriage, though blessed with fine children and economic advantages, had simply not turned out like she had imagined. She could, it was true, buy all the jewellery and expensive clothes she wanted, travel the world, afford the most extravagant of entertainments. And yet she remained somehow unfulfilled. She had sometimes wondered why she had married him, for she was convinced that she no longer loved him. Perhaps it was only circumstances that had pushed them together and she had never really loved him.

She could not remember at what point she had started becoming jealous and resentful of his work. His late nights at the office, the sheer exhilaration of making or losing a fortune in a matter of minutes, and his urgent trips to New York or London or Zurich for consultations and strategy meetings, all smacked of the kind of excitement that life should be made up of.

But she had no part in that. She could not imagine how he could soak up all that economic data for forward positions and futures contracts, sense arbitrage opportunities, exploit cross-currency interest differentials and yet remain oblivious to her needs. He probably would not recognize her needs even if they hit him between the eyes. To cap it all, he had to get himself killed and condemn her to a widowhood for which she was totally unprepared.

In bygone days Chinese widows were supposed to bear such misfortunes with loyalty and fortitude. If they remained unquestionably chaste, they could look forward to memorial arches being erected in their honour. But she did not give two hoots for memorial arches. What really upset her was the damnable prospect of an enforced celibacy at the age of forty-five! She could, of course, remarry but there was not a remotely suitable man in sight. As for other alternatives, they were just too sordid for words.

She was glad that, following the funeral, the rest of the family had dispersed back to where they belonged — the twins to their micro-electronics jobs in Southern California, along with their wives, and Sharon to her junior year at Bryn Mawr. That at least gave her peace and quiet to figure an escape from her embarrassing situation.

A few years ago it would have outraged Hannah if someone had suggested that she harboured a hunger for carnal pleasures. After all, she was a well brought up Chinese girl and well brought up Chinese girls were not supposed to think about such things, let alone to seek enjoyment from them. They were supposed to remain passive, to submit with resignation to their husbands' cruder instincts. If, in the course of things, they were driven to those shuddering heights of unmentionable sensations, then they should grit their teeth or bite their lips rather than let loose shrieks of animal abandonment. To behave otherwise would be to debase their entire upbringing, to reduce them to the level of sing-song girls and loose women.

Thus, throughout the early years of her marriage, Hannah had felt an acute sense of guilt, which prevented her from enjoying to the full Chai's unbridled passions. He had led her into dark areas of sensual experience, which frightened her because they stirred in her a shameful and terrifying enjoyment. Later, when she tried to curb those disgusting yearnings, she found herself suffering from quick flares of temper, persistent irritabilities and a propensity to laugh and giggle too much over quite inconsequential jokes.

She tried to justify those quirks to herself in terms of having married too young, of being straddled too soon with the responsibilities of motherhood, and of upsetting the flow of her hormones through birth control. If those explanations proved unconvincing, she would throw in the obstreperousness of the children and the sheer stupidity of the servants.

It was only many years later, after the fierce waves of women's liberation pounded upon Asian shores, that she finally identified the repression of her feminine sensuality as the cause of her prickliness and began sloughing off her inhibitions. But by that time she was already approaching forty and Chai had lost his drive and his taste for sexual experimentations. Her marriage thus became little more than a civilized social shell within which to hide her smouldering desires. That facade became even more intolerable after the children left.

Without the children to distract her, she was left to simmer with a slow, secret frustration, a frustration only hinted at by the dark rings of passion around her eyes. The insistent hunger in her loins kept reminding her of how she was being starved and deprived. But the mental habits of a lifetime prevented her from broaching the subject directly with Chai. She felt the whole business beneath her.

Temptations of the flesh, at her age, was a vice which would find little sympathy and understanding at her level in Chinese society, especially when her children would soon be conferring upon her the status of grandmother! But on the other hand, the needs of her body could not be denied. Although her figure was showing the signs of middle age plumpness and some strategic places were not as firm as she would like, she thought it was still well proportioned and attractive. Indeed, when she wore formal attire, her décolletage could still draw the admiring glances of men of the world like Mike Sullivan. But in spite of decking herself out in nightdresses of the flimsiest black lace, Chai hardly noticed.

Once, in another attempt to rekindle his fire, she had actually placed on the bedside table a copy of the *Kama Sutra*, illustrated with pictures of the explicit carvings in the temples of Konarak and Khajuraho. But Chai had merely flipped through the illustrations, muttered "Crazy Hindoos!" and promptly went to sleep.

Having finished with the drawers, Hannah got up to tackle the Chubb safe. Chai had told her exactly what it would contain. Inside would be their stock and share certificates, the title deed to their home, insurance policies for the cars, the home, Sharon's education and his own life, his cheque books and some traveller's cheques. She took those items out one by one and put them into her large handbag.

To her surprise she also found also a bundle of letters in an unfamiliar hand. With a sense of foreboding she picked up the letters. Chai had never been much of a letter writer, even where the children were concerned, and such a large bundle of letters implied a lively correspondence. She took the letters back to the desk and hesitated for a moment before reading them. As she did so she turned pale and began to tremble. They were love letters addressed to Chai from a woman — apparently American and obviously vulgar — by the name of Kay!

Interlaced with usual drooling of lovers were passages of revelation. "I had no idea Oriental men were so cool, much more interesting than Americans," one of them read. "It's really neat when you explain our relationship in terms of the Yin and the Yang, of merging our duality in cosmic unity. It beats talking dirty! I guess Eastern cultures must know a thing or two!"

A passage from another letter went: "I get what you mean when you say that all grief stems from love. How sad and how beautiful! I miss you terribly, whenever I receive one of your letters or hear your voice on the telephone. Meeting only once every few months is more than I can bear. I am trying my best to accept your point of view that love is an intoxication, a flight of fancy, whereas marriage is a dreary journey between boredom and ennui. But if so, why keep making that journey with a bitchy woman you do not love?"

Yet another letter read: "Thanks for the trip to Zurich. Although we only had two days, they were great. You Asians seem to have a name for everything. Fancy an 'embrace of the jaghana' and 'the sporting of a sparrow'! They are simply out of this world! I'll never remember all the names but I'm looking forward to more! Don't let old sourpuss get you down."

Hannah could not go on. She crumpled the letters up with both her hands as bitter tears coursed down her face. She recognized the terms from the *Kama Sutra* and realized on a sudden that what Chai had been calling out in his sleep might well have been "Oh, Kay! Oh, Kay!" She flung the crumpled letters into the wastepaper basket with all her strength and let out a mighty wail.

Mike Sullivan must have heard her from his office next door for he soon knocked and came into the room. "Oh, Hannah! I know this must be very distressing for you," he said, his voice full of sympathy. "Why don't you let me take you home?"

Hannah looked at Mike Sullivan standing tall, blond and virile before her. "Yes, yes," she sobbed as she allowed herself to be led away.

"Aftershock" has appeared in *The Peak* magazine in Hong Kong.

A Good Day for Dying

Szechuen has few rivals in China for the sheer splendour of its spring. Its dark green mountains and lush valleys, alive with the colours of rhododendrons, camellias, oleanders and azaleas, challenged the imagination with shifting moods, appearing at times misty and contemplative and at other times resplendent with sunlight. Stately pines, gnarled cypresses and pliant bamboos flourished, together with apples, apricots, bananas, loquats, papayas and sweet cherries. As if that were not enough, almonds, tea bushes and fat juicy tomatoes added to the profusion. The buzz of honeybees and the flutterings of butterflies garnished nature's abundance. It was small wonder ancient bearers of tribute from Tibet, Nepal and other faraway places often assumed Szechuen to be some hidden paradise they had stumbled upon en route to the Chinese capital.

Cheng Yin sat with his back against a camphor tree, taking in the scene. He was a strapping lad, whose steady eyes, resolute mouth and determined jaw insinuated a certain stubbornness of character. The mingled fragrances of fruits and flowers held him and he marvelled at the abundance of orchards, bamboo groves and giant ratten creepers. It was the end of May, yet the air still tingled with the crispness of spring.

He was not knowledgeable about plants and flowers. He could not assign names to the delicate blues, the bashful pinks and the teasing yellows dotting the craggy hills. An intermittent breeze danced fitfully, brushing his lean face as playfully as a flirting woman. He was thankful he was alive on such a day and at such a place. He wanted to store away the pleasure of the moment, for he doubted he would ever come this way again.

No sooner had he admitted that thought, he felt a tingle of shame. He should not take pleasure from the bountifulness of nature. The Communist Party had drummed into him that sentimentality was a habit of the feudal past. It made for weakness. A son of the Revolution could not afford to be weak.

Cheng Yin was dressed in the shapeless uniform of the Red Army, with a cloth cap worn jauntily at the back of his head. His feet sported a pair of worn straw sandals. Like the other twenty-one members of the Second Company of the Fourth Shock Regiment selected for the assault on Luting Bridge, he had a broadsword strapped to his back and a supply of hand grenades attached to his belt. While most of the others were also equipped with tommy guns, he preferred the trusty Mauser by his side, snug in its leather holster.

He and his comrades had arrived less than an hour ago, after marching all night. Their battalion commander had rewarded them with a good meal and most of the others were dozing.

"You should snatch some sleep," the company commander said, as he passed among the men. "We attack at four."

The company commander was called Old Yeh. He had unusually prominent cheekbones and a pointed chin. The hollowness of his cheeks, occasioned by months of under-nourishment and repeated forced marches, combined with his other features to shape the face in the form of a quaint, inverted triangle. That unlikely physiognomy was livened by a pair of ardent eyes which lent it the dreamy air of an intellectual turned revolutionary. He was only twenty-five but among the illiterate peasant youngsters making up the bulk of the Red Army he was considered an "elder".

"I'm not sleepy," Cheng Yin replied.

Old Yeh sat down next to Cheng Yin. "I know what you're thinking," he said. His voice was cultured and well-modulated. "Things will be different this time. Future generations will remember what we are about to achieve."

They were bosom friends and had seen much action together. Both were educated men, steeped in history and legends, and both knew that this idyllic setting had been the location for some horrendous blood-lettings. During the period of the Warring States, two thousand four hundred years ago, legendary armies had fought epic battles and perished here. Just seventy years ago, 40,000 Taiping rebels had been trapped and slaughtered on the banks of the Tatu River by the armies of the Ching Emperor. But neither could give voice to such chilling knowledge. Their comrades were a superstitious lot, and any hint of past carnages at that spot would completely destroy their faith in the success of their mission.

"Look at us," Cheng Yin said, lowering his voice to a whisper. "We marched out of southern Kiangsi last October with a force of eighty or ninety thousand. Now we are down to barely twenty thousand. Too much blood has already been spilt. And for what? We don't even know where we're heading. We're running around like dogs chasing their own tails. Do our leaders really know what they're about? Do they have a plan? Rumours are rife, of serious disagreements between our leaders and the foreigner from the Comintern. And all the while the enemy is closing in, hammering us. We are like sitting ducks."

"That's why we must capture Luting Bridge," Old Yeh whispered back. "We must have faith. If we believe in the Revolution we must carry on, through thick and thin. Circumstances are against us. That bridge provides our only means of escape. The future of the Revolution rests upon its capture and the Second Company has been chosen for the honour."

Cheng Yin snorted. "Twenty-two men leading a suicide attack! We don't even know what's waiting for us on the other side! There may be hundreds of defenders. What we know for sure is that they've got two machine guns, perhaps also mortars."

"Have faith. I'll be right there with you. Intelligence reports suggest that, apart from the machine guns, the defenders are armed only with antiquated rifles. Once we've knocked out the machine guns, the rest should be easy. It's a good day for fame and glory. Take a rest. You'll need all the energy you have. I've got things to attend to."

After Old Yeh had left, Cheng Yin allowed himself to contemplate the unthinkable. Should the Second Company fail, the lazy, sun-splashed day might well turn out to be a good one for dying. He could visualize his comrades being cut down on the banks of the Tatu River just like the Taiping rebels seventy years earlier. Always so much blood being traded for so many beguiling dreams!

He had no fear of death. In the three years since joining the Red Army he had seen enough of it to last many lifetimes. Everyone had to die, sooner or later. It all boiled down to how. One could perish like a gnat, squashed between the fingers of fate, or one could go like a man, shouting defiance at the sky. His only regret was that he never told his unhappy father that he loved him. Now it was too late.

His father was a man of education, who knew the difference between right and wrong. The problem was that the poor man could never stand up for what was right or lead the life he desired. Working as a rent collector for an absentee landlord was deeply repugnant to his instincts. Yet he lacked the will to cast aside the comfortable living and the opium pipe that came with it. He was fearful of inflicting hardship upon his son and sought escape through the pipe

Cheng Yin would not have minded hardship. What he could not stand was to see his father being sorrowful and sad. As a child he had often gone with his father on rent collecting missions, escorted by two bodyguards, both experts with sword and staff. At first he enjoyed those trips because they took him to places he had never seen and because the bodyguards gave him lessons in kung fu during stop-overs on their journeys.

But as he grew older the crushing poverty of the peasants in the arid uplands of Anhui troubled him. They seemed aged before their time, worlds away from the wealth, the servants, the opium couches and the chirpy young concubines at the home of his father's employer. When he went with his father to deliver the accumulated takings, those pretty, giggling women used to ruffle his hair and pinch his cheeks. The sweetmeats they offered had seemed an exceptional treat at first. Afterwards he regarded their touch and their gifts as unclean.

Gradually he lost respect for the bodyguards too. He did not like the way they shouted at the peasants and threatened them physically. Their behaviour violated his notions of chivalry which those engaged in the martial arts ought to uphold.

On the other hand, his love and respect for his father grew. He caught his father surreptitiously slipping coins to peasants heavily in debt, only to go through the motion later of taking them back as rent in front of the bodyguards. Such discoveries led him to run away at the age of sixteen, in order to free his father from responsibility for providing for him.

Had his gesture made any difference? Had his father ceased to live like a gnat? It would be comforting to know before the attack the bridge began.

The whine of enemy mortar suddenly cut across his reflections. Two shells had been lobbed from across the river. One landed harmlessly on a patch of irises but the second found a kitchen detail arranging provisions for the next meal. One cook was killed and two others slightly wounded.

Pandemonium broke out among the resting men. Some yelled for medics. Others rushed for cover.

"Shit! They've got mortars!" someone yelled.

The death inflicted upon a non-combatant without reason enraged the men. Those manning mortars wanted to respond. But the battalion commander stopped them. "You'll get your revenge soon enough," he said. "Just calm down. We can't afford to damage the bridge. That is the sole consideration at this stage."

From his vantage point Cheng Yin examined Luting Bridge again. It was a single-span construction of about a hundred yards long, built almost two and a half centuries ago during the reign of Emperor Kang Hsi. It consisted of thirteen giant iron chains with links of more than five inches in diameter. The chains were embedded into great stone buttresses hidden inside red bridge houses with jaunty curved roofs on both sides of the river.

Nine of the chains had been set in a parallel pattern, held together at regular intervals by metal bars. They supported heavy wooden boards, which formed the floor of the bridge. Two further chains on either side, set higher and connected with palings, served as crude guard-rails.

Four hundred feet below the bridge raged the turbulent Tatu River. It tumbled down from the highlands of Chinghai and was at that point squeezed between dark jagged cliffs. That natural constriction caused it to seethe with whirlpools and vicious cross-currents. The agonized wailing of wind tearing to escape from the canyons provided a chilling accompaniment. Crossing the bridge was a dizzying and unnerving experience. It swayed like a hammock.

Those assigned to capture the bridge, however, could not count on the luxury of crossing on a wooden floor. The defenders had removed two-thirds of the boards, leaving seventy yards of naked chains as the only means of reaching the other side. Hostile fire was also a given.

As the hour set for the assault approached, Old Yeh assembled the team and went over the plan again. The men selected to lead the attack would crawl along the chains under cover of the battalion's heavy machine guns. The rest of the company, together with the Third Company, would follow, placing fresh boards on the bridge as fast as possible. The priority was to destroy the two machine gun nests and to hold the bridge till reinforcements got over.

A Good Day for Dying

As Cheng Yin listened to Old Yeh he slowly re-adjusted his cap. He knew at least some — if not all of them — would never see the end of the day. He hoped their deaths would not be as pointless as that of the poor cooks or of the tens of thousands who had already perished during the months of running skirmishes.

At precisely four o'clock the blare of bugles pierced the air. The martial notes sounding the charge stirred the blood. Cheng Yin raced forward and became the first to climb onto a chain. As he crawled along he heard encouragements being shouted by the rest of the battalion, accompanied by the cheerful chatter of supporting fire. By comparison, the responding fire sounded insipid, like the distant poppings of mouldy firecrackers.

The bridge swayed erratically as more and more men clambered onto its skeleton. Suddenly, the chains, which had previously seemed so massive, became like flimsy threads in a spider's web, with the men clinging to them like trapped flies.

After Cheng Yin had proceeded forty yards along his chain, the whizz of incoming bullets sounded more sharp and threatening. Then, without warning, a terrifying scream rent the air, receding in heart-stopping echoes into the depths of the canyon. It was followed quickly by another anguished cry. At the same time the metal web of the bridge tossed and bucked furiously.

Two of his comrades had fallen, either hit or slipped. Cheng Yin hung on desperately, trying to retain his balance and to ride out the swaying. Nausea welled up in him. His eyes, normally so bright and uncompromising, dimmed vertiginously. He seemed no longer in control of his muscles. He froze on his chain.

"Don't look down! Keep moving!" a voice snapped at him from close by. It was Old Yeh.

The familiar voice steadied him. "I'm all right. Just go ahead. Nothing's wrong," he replied, panting.

His hands were sweating profusely and the links of the chain had become slippery under their grasp. He strengthened the grip on the chain with his thighs before taking one hand off to dry its palm on his trousers. Then he repeated the procedure with the other hand.

In the process he noticed a few comrades had already moved well ahead of him on their respective chains. He inhaled deeply to clear his dizziness. He had no fear of dying. He had counted on a swift soldier's death, however, not a prolonged and agonizing ordeal suspended in mid-air. To fall screaming from a great height would rob his death of dignity.

After he had recovered his composure he resumed the journey. When he was about fifteen yards from the remaining boards, he saw flames leaping up. The defenders had set the boards alight with kerosene, in a desperate attempt to thwart the attack.

The first of his team had already mounted the boards. That sight, together with the leaping flames, exhilarated him. He knew the ordeal was almost over. He covered the remaining distance in a fury of energy. Once on the boarded part of the bridge, he drew his Mauser with one hand and unclasped a grenade with the other.

"Sha! Sha! Sha!" he yelled, as he charged towards the smoke and flames.

Others took up the cry. The sound of "Kill! Kill! Kill!" reverberated all around.

He fired his Mauser as he ran and when he was within throwing distance he launched grenade after grenade. As he charged through the flames he knew that success was almost within reach. But before he could unclasp another grenade, he felt something strange happening to his legs. He crashed down onto the burning boards and hit his head with great force.

He felt no pain, however, as he crashed onto the burning boards. He was only aware of flames licking at his clothes. In that one brief, devastating moment before slipping consciousness he smiled. He knew he was not going to die like a gnat.

"A Good Day for Dying" has appeared in *The New Writer* in Britain.

Lost River

It was one of those glorious July days that came all too infrequently during the English summer, and Jasmine took it as a special welcome to mark her return to London after more than thirty years. She luxuriated in the brilliant sunshine as she strolled from the Savoy, past the crowds on the Strand and down towards the Embankment.

A few heads turned upon her passing. The fact that she could still produce such an effect at the age of fifty gave her a momentary glow of satisfaction. Her smooth skin and her black hair, gathered in a stylish chignon, certainly disguised her age, while the designer dress from Harrods showed to advantage her small, trim figure. A necklace of Mikimoto pearls conferred an additional touch of elegance. But it was really her deportment that was arresting. There was a certain majesty in her carriage, with every movement feline and supple and a joy to behold. That kind of grace could only have come from long training as a ballet dancer.

On reaching the Embankment, Jasmine followed the walkway alongside the Thames. The placid river was shimmering with sunlight and a light river breeze brushed her like a whispering caress. It was a day in which a person ought to be bursting with the joy of being alive. And yet she was being bothered by an unsettling ambivalence. It was as if she had some pressing task to complete and yet dreaded getting down to it. Thus her stroll seemed an evasion.

She had taken that same aimless walk for the past three days, ever since Pong went home to leave her to that extra week in London she wanted. If she did not sort herself out quickly, she would go out of her mind.

After a while Jasmine stopped, as she had done on previous days, and leaned her arms against the thick stone wall bordering the river. The fingers of one hand played with her string of pearls. Her tilted, Oriental eyes gazed for a long while at nothing in particular, hardly taking in the luminous sky, the traffic plying the river or the slight river haze rendering indistinct the buildings on the far bank.

When her dark eyes rested upon the graceful arches of Waterloo Bridge in the middle distance, they took on a preoccupied look and her mind zoomed back to the distant past. Her generous mouth broke into an ironical smile. How much water must have flowed beneath that bridge since her last visit, she thought. She had been right to stay away. London contained too many memories, too many ghosts. After more than thirty years they still had the power to unsettle her and to play havoc with her emotions.

No one in her circle of friends quite understood her reluctance to visit London. She had refused all explanation, leaving them to their own surmises. Some had ascribed to her a dislike for the fog and the damp, others an aversion to English food. Still others put it down to her dismal student days. She allowed them their speculations and kept her own counsel.

Even Pong, before flying back to Hong Kong, chided her by saying: "Ever since I have known you, you have refused to visit London. You did not want to come as part of our honeymoon, you did not want to come to put the children in school and university, you did not want to make it any part of our holidays in Europe. One would have thought the Black Death was still stalking its streets.

"And now, when we've finally persuaded you to come for Charity's graduation, you suddenly want to extend your stay without explanation. If you had told me earlier, I could have re-arranged my schedule. Now I have to leave you on your own. I'll never understand women."

"It'll only be for a week," she had replied. "I'll be home soon enough. Don't worry."

Standing there beside the Thames, Jasmine pondered again her restlessness over the last three days. Why had she given way so suddenly to the impulse to remain? She had no friends to see, no unfinished shopping to attend to. And yet the urge to remain had been so compelling that she was impatient for Pong to be gone. What was she hoping to experience or discover or achieve? She did not know. If she could not find an answer for herself, how could she explain to others?

London, of course, was the most beloved of all the cities she had known. She had gone there at the fervent age of sixteen to enroll at Sadler's Wells, as the Royal Ballet was then called. For three years it had been an enchanted place where dreams of artistic success, happiness and love had blossomed like flowers, where on a certain enchanted evening she had attained that status known as womanhood. But it was the bittersweet memories of what happened thereafter that now held her to the city.

For more than three decades she had guarded those memories against all comers, relegating them to the level of the subconscious. But now they were intruding upon her willy-nilly, completely out of control.

Perhaps the old sights and sounds of London were responsible. Charity's graduation and her departure for a European holiday with her fiancé were also to blame. They suddenly made her realize the best part of her life was over and done with and left her wondering what it had amounted to.

She had been a dutiful daughter, a faithful wife and a loving mother. Had that been enough to counterbalance the evasions and surrenders pressing so uncomfortably upon her conscience? If so, why that bitter nostalgia for what Arnold called the "youth-time" of her life? If not, then what else must a woman do to find peace?

Ever since she could remember, the only thing she desired was to dance. Soon after the war, when she was nine, her parents had enrolled her for ballet lessons in the belief that ballet was good for a girl's posture.

She soon found she could express herself in a dance in a way she never could with words. Her progress had been so exceptional that Mrs. Rubinovich, her Russian teacher, persuaded her parents to send her to Sadler's Wells for further training.

Mrs. Rubinovich also arranged as her guardian a woman of ancient vintage, Eastern European origins and formidable proportions. But apart from settling her into a boarding-house, which suited her modest circumstances and inviting her to an occasional meal, the guardian rarely intruded into her life. She was thus left to fend largely for herself in an alien city, which had taken a month by boat to reach.

Her first weeks in London were a period of utter misery. She could not get used to boarding-house food nor the necessity of sharing a communal bathroom. Her fellow boarders were for the most part students but there was not a ballet dancer among them. They were too boisterous to suit her disposition and their horseplay and shrill laughter got on her nerves. She felt utterly wretched until Arnold Beresford made friends with her and introduced her to the endless delights of London.

She had met Arnold by chance, when they both turned up late for dinner at the boarding-house one evening. They were the sole occupants of the dining room and sat across from each other as plates of cold sausages and mashed potatoes were dumped before them. Then their eyes met and they both burst out laughing at their common misery. From that moment onwards, Arnold assumed the role of guide, advisor and friend.

Arnold was two years her senior and was one of the few non-students living in the boarding-house. He had sandy-coloured hair, ardent blue eyes and a resolute jaw with an attractive cleft at the bottom of his chin. There was an air of purpose about him, which set him apart from the other boarders.

He was from Doncaster and was the son of a coal miner. He seemed to have tried his hand at an incredible number of jobs. He had started by delivering milk in a horse-drawn cart. Then, because he developed an interest in horses, he became a stable boy for a year. At the time they met, he was working as a sales assistant at Bennington, that venerable firm which had provided sensible footwear for British gentlefolk for more than a hundred years.

But he indicated his real mission in life was to become a writer and regarded everything he had done or was doing as a preparation for his chosen calling. His clear ambition and determination to succeed filled her with admiration.

Arnold saw to it that she savoured everything London had to offer. He made a point of showing her the paintings and sculptures by Degas. She took to them immediately, for they seemed to express the essence of the life she sought. She could easily imagine herself posing for each of the works, in a basic position, exercising at the barre or simply lacing up a ballet shoe.

Arnold, as if reading her thoughts, had then said in his low, earnest voice: "You could be better than any of them. You could be a Chinese Pavlova or Ulanova. All you have to do is to want it desperately enough."

"Oh, I have never aimed so high," she had replied. "I just want to dance. I should be quite happy dancing in an ensemble."

"You must not short-change yourself. You must have ambition. When you set out to do something you must aim to be the best. There is nothing sadder than to see talent going to waste, since so few of us are really talented. You are talented. You have been endowed with a gift and, as its possessor, you have a duty to perfect it and bring some beauty into this dismal world of ours."

No one had spoken to her in such a way before. Hitherto, her sheltered existence as the only daughter of a small textile manufacturer had led her to believe that dancing was just a passing indulgence. It was something to be enjoyed before assuming the burdens of adulthood, of helping in the family business, and of finding a husband and raising children.

Arnold's exposition had given her a fresh point of reference. Thereafter she did her barre exercises with heightened enthusiasm, conscious that every perfectly executed pirouette or entrechat quatre had the power to brighten the world. That new awareness was the first of many that Arnold was to bring into her life.

Her association with him soon settled into a pattern. From Monday to Saturday, they would have dinner together. After dinner, he invariably retired to his room, to follow a strict regime of reading and writing. He advised her to devise a similar schedule for herself.

Sunday was the day for fun. They would spend it together, wandering around London or visiting nearby places like Greenwich, Windsor and Bath. They would make their plans over dinner during the previous week and their obvious contentment in each other's company soon caused them to be dubbed "the turtle-doves".

Such teasing by other boarders drove her to the verge of tears on more than one occasion, for it carried the implication that her relationship with Arnold was less than innocent. Since she was thirteen, her mother had impressed upon her the need for a girl to be chaste and those exhortations had been emphasized more forcefully prior to her departure for England. Her mother kept repeating the lines from the Odes:

"A man may do a wrong, and Time
Will fling its cloak to hide his crime:
A woman who has lost her name
Is doomed to everlasting shame."

She had often trembled at the thought that her feelings towards Arnold might contain more than friendship. She could neither explain those feelings nor give them a name. All she knew was that she felt comfortable and safe in his company and derived a peculiar pleasure if he so much as allowed her to sew a button or darn a sock for him. When he failed to turn up for dinner, she would become unaccountably lost and she would tingle with curiosity whenever she thought of what he might be doing each evening locked up in his room.

Once she asked to see some of his writing but Arnold replied: "You'll read them soon enough, when the world is ready for me. But if I don't make it, why bother with the scribblings of a failure?"

On the contrary, she wanted to share everything with Arnold. It pleased her enormously when Arnold took an interest in different aspects of her development. He would correct her faulty pronunciations or her wrong usage of idioms. He would recommend books for her to read, music for her to enjoy and ideas for her to ponder. He took particular interest in her progress as a dancer and sometimes asked her to improvise outrageous dances like "a radio suffering from static interference" or "the metamorphosis of a character out of Kafka or Dostoyevsky".

"Dancing is more than just mastering sets of steps. Every mother's child knows how to dance like sylphs or dying swans," he once told her. "For it to become real art you need to find a unique way of expressing what people have been struggling to express. Nothing else is worth a damn."

In order to live up to his expectations, she redoubled her efforts to perfect her dancing. Then, one day, he suddenly began addressing her as "Dancer" and she knew her progress had met with his approval.

Jasmine smiled to herself in recalling those days. Wonderful things never seemed to last, she thought. One day you were young and innocent and in no time at all you were old. It was so unfair.

She turned away from the river and crossed over to the small park on the other side of the road. She walked the length of the park and back again. When she came to an unoccupied bench in the shade, she sat down and felt refreshed by the subtle coolness of the shade.

Trying to re-live the past was a stupid exercise, she told herself. If she continued on her present tack, all she would find nothing but memories of pain, of lost opportunities, of surrenders and regrets. Yet, somehow, she knew she had to press on, to confront her past and come to terms with it. If purging the past was necessary, what better place was there than the very city where the most traumatic events took place?

Jasmine took herself back again to her final year at Sadler's Wells. She remembered how attached to Arnold she had become by that time. It seemed that so long as she could dance and enjoy his company that would be the acme of happiness.

She recalled her apprehension on the approach of graduation. Unless a miracle happened, that would mean the end of her stay in London. That prospect filled her with desperation. She knew it was possible for students doing well to enter the school's ballet company after graduation. Without so much as pausing for thought, she applied for a position.

"You've done very well, my dear, and I'm exceptionally pleased with your progress," her teacher said. "You're a superb little dancer but I'm afraid it's going to be difficult to find you a place."

"Am I not as good as the others?" Jasmine asked.

"Oh, no, no! Quite the contrary. You're better than most. But you see, my dear, it is not only dancing that counts. You also have to fit in."

"I don't understand."

"Well, my dear, try to imagine yourself in an ensemble or a chorus. Can't you see that you will not blend well? You're smaller than the other girls. And then there is your Asiatic face. One dark face among all those pale ones. It just won't work, don't you see?'

"I only want to continue dancing."

"Why not go home and join one of the companies there?"

"There are no ballet companies in Hong Kong."

"Well, there's your chance to start one."

She had returned to the boarding-house devastated. When she recounted the episode to Arnold amidst a flood of tears, he was indignant.

"What do those old fogies know?" Arnold demanded. "That's the trouble with us British. We cling to a constipated life. We stick with what our grandfathers are accustomed to. We don't realize the world is changing. Hell! In America all kinds of new dance forms are evolving. Size and colour don't matter two hoots. Don't worry, we can shake the dust off this place. We'll go to New York and show the world what can be done."

That evening, because of her distress, Arnold allowed her into his room and as he comforted her the inevitable happened. Arnold declared his love, causing all the pent-up affection she felt for him to burst forth. She forgot about her mother's admonitions, about the Odes, and surrendered herself.

Thereafter, staying at the boarding-house and sneaking into each other's room became intolerable. Arnold urged her to move into a place of their own. But she was hesitant.

"Look, this is the youth-time of our lives," Arnold argued. "It is a time for following the dictates of our hearts. Life will force us into retreats and surrenders soon enough. But in the youth-time of our lives we can defy the world and make of life what we will."

Shortly thereafter, they moved into a small flat and the two or three months that followed were the happiest in her life.

But news had a way of travelling thousands of miles, especially when one did not particularly want it to spread. Before she knew it her father was in London, demanding that she pack her bags for home. Those terrible three-cornered scenes, with the two men she loved shouting incomprehensibly at each other, remained as vividly as if they had happened yesterday. No effort by her could soften the sharp edges in their exchanges.

"Have you no shame?" her father demanded, in a voice filled with both sorrow and anger. "How can you take up with a common salesman?"

"He's not a salesman, Father," she tried to explain through her tears. "He aims to be a writer. He's still trying to learn about life."

"Then let him learn with someone else's daughter! Your mother has been sick with worrying since she heard what you've been up to."

"I'm sorry Mother had to learn of it that way. But we love each other."

"Love? What do you know about love? You're just in your teens."

"What's going on?" Arnold interjected, catching the anger and frustration in the voices. "Tell him we want to get married."

After she had interpreted, her father replied: "You think marriage will solve everything? How will you live? You're our only child. Are you going to remain ten thousand miles away? What would be the difference then between having a child and having none?"

"We could come to live in Hong Kong," she suggested, desperately.

"And what would this man do in Hong Kong? Sell shoes? He does not speak our language. He does not know our customs. He may not even like our food. Will he just sit there when relatives gather on festive days? And when you have children, am I supposed to take them to the park and explain to all and sundry why my grandchildren have blue eyes and fair hair? If you have any consideration at all for your mother or for myself you will pack your things this instant."

As her tears tumbled down in torrents, Arnold kept demanding: "What's he saying? What's he saying?"

She avoided interpreting the worst of her father's outburst and simply said: "I have to go home. My mother is sick and is asking for me. I owe her a duty to go back."

"I'm sorry to learn of your mother's illness," Arnold said. "But let us get married first. Then we can both go to see her."

"No, you don't understand. I am Chinese. Chinese girls have to get their parents' permission before getting married. My father is upset now. But when I get home I can explain things to him and to my mother. Please be patient and trust me. I will come back to you very soon."

"How soon?"

"A few months. A year at the most."

"No! If you leave I know I'll lose you. I love you and don't want to lose you. Can't you see we have our own lives to live? We can't be governed by what parents want. Confucius has been dead for twenty-four centuries. It's time we buried him. Let us just go and get married. Things can sort themselves out afterwards."

"That's impossible. You just don't understand."

"Yes, I do understand! I understand better than you. Listen to me, Dancer. What you decide today will seal both our fates forever. So listen very carefully. Your parents mean well but they cannot live your life for you. Only you can do that. You must know that you if go back, your parents will never let you return here. And I haven't got the money to come to you. It will mean the end of both your dancing and our love.

"Don't you realize what we are both facing today is our Rubicon, our river of no return? You see, there is something very peculiar about rivers. A river never remains the same because fresh waters are flowing into it all the time. Therefore no on can cross the same river twice. We are now on the edge of our special river. We either cross it together or we lose it forever.

"If we fail to cross, then that something which makes you want to dance and makes me want to write will die. If that happens, then we might as well be dead too. We may go on breathing and eating and talking but for all intents and purposes we will be dead. So let's cross our river together now."

"I can't! I can't!" she wailed.

Jasmine looked up at the sunlight filtering through the tracery of leaves and suddenly realized that she had been crying. She took out a handkerchief of fine Irish liner and dabbed her eyes.

Yes, Arnold had been right, she thought. Something died that day and everything thereafter turned colourless and flat. She wrote numerous letters to declare her love and to plead for patience but Arnold never replied. After more than a year she stopped writing.

Then relatives introduced her to Pong, an architect at the start of his career. Pong never enthused about any mission in life the way Arnold did. He just had a knack for designing buildings, which maximized plot ratios and squeezed out every last bit of useable space. Developers loved him. She eventually married him for want of anything better to do. Although Pong provided her with all the luxuries she could possibly want, their years of marriage passed like grey shadows, one indistinguishable from another.

Now her parents were dead and her children had grown up. Her son had become an architect and had acquired his father's designing talents. Charity had just graduated from the University of Manchester with a dentistry degree. She would happily spend the rest of her days straightening teeth and filling cavities. It was strange that both her children had opted for careers that were safe and practical. They would never be troubled by yearnings of the spirit or lose sleep over intractable human issues.

Jasmine speculated momentarily whether she would have made anything of her dancing if she had gone to New York with Arnold. She had a failure of nerve at the crucial time and now she would never know.

But what of Arnold? Did he remain true to his destiny or did his divine spark die as well? If he had carried on writing she would feel less guilty about her own failure. Through the years she had kept an eye out for books bearing his name but found none. She comforted herself with the thought he might have used a pseudonym.

All of a sudden she felt an overwhelming need to know. She realized at once that was the real purpose of her extended stay. But how could one go about locating someone after more than thirty years? Well, Bennington had been in existence for over a hundred years and that was as good a place as any to start. So thinking, she got up from the bench to make her way back to the Savoy.

It took her half an hour of telephoning to discover that old staff records were kept at Bennington's headquarters in Birmingham. Several calls later she got through to the Personnel Manager.

"I'm terribly sorry to trouble you," Jasmine told the woman at the other end of the line, "but I'm wondering if you could help me with a personal matter. I'm from abroad and I'm anxious to locate an old friend who used to work for Bennington thirty years ago. I know this is a long shot but I thought you might have a forwarding address or something to help me pick up the trail."

"We do keep records for a fair while but thirty years in a very long time. I'll see what I can do. What is your friend's name and where did he work?"

"When I knew him he was a sales clerk at the Piccadilly branch of Bennington. His name was Arnold Beresford."

"Oh, goodness gracious me!" the voice at the other end exclaimed with a laugh. "Mr. Beresford is still with us! He's now our Sales Director. I'm sure he will be delighted to hear from an old friend. Unfortunately, he's out of the country at the moment. Summer vacation, you know. He'll be back in a fortnight. If you would leave a message I'll see that Mr. Beresford gets it."

An image of Arnold flashed across Jasmine's mind. It was an image of a stout, greying businessman with a gold watch chain strung across his waistcoat, leaving a house in suburbia to catch the 8.15, absorbed with the weekly sales figures and the schedule for the stores promotion. Her heart felt like a stone within her breast.

"No, there's no message," Jasmine said to the telephone. "Now that I know where he is I can get hold of him when he returns. Thank you very much."

Jasmine heard the receiver being replaced at the other end. She lowered her own instrument onto her lap and sat holding the dead telephone for a very long time.

"Lost River" has appeared in *Discovery* magazine in Hong Kong and *Short Story International* in the United States.

Coil of the Serpent

I was halfway towards my seventh birthday when malaria claimed the life of my mother. Inhabitants of our crumbling tenement had long complained about mosquitoes breeding in an adjacent lot abandoned by failed developers. It took the death of my mother to gain the attention of health authorities, represented by half a dozen men wearing khaki uniforms and white facemasks. They had canisters strapped to their backs, from which they sprayed a mist through metal prods upon the stagnant puddles and the rainwater trapped in discarded food and kerosene cans.

The passing of my mother was a baffling experience, not at all as I had imagined death to be. She had been shivering in bed for days though her skin remained hot to the touch. When she stopped shivering I thought she had gone to sleep. I did not want to trouble her for dinner so I scrounged something from our food cupboard. When she failed to stir by the following evening, I tried to wake her. She smelt different, like dirty clothes, and her skin was cold. I realized something had gone terribly wrong and cried for help.

After my mother's body had been removed by ambulance attendants, neighbours gave some rice and fish to eat, but I had no appetite. I sat around our tight little room just holding the plate of food most of that night, not knowing what to do until my father returned. I didn't know how long that might be because my father was a travelling salesman. He seldom appeared more than once every two or three weeks. No one knew how to contact him. In the event he showed up two days later.

I had little idea what kind of travelling salesman he was. He had a brown cardboard suitcase from which he brought out beads and ribbons, lipsticks and nylon stockings, ointments for pimples and powders for athlete's foot. He often boasted of making big money one day and promised my mother a splendid house across the causeway in Singapore. The fact my mother would never get to see that dream house troubled me. We had often talked about it in our room, amidst the smells of other people's food and other people's lives. She told me things would be different once we had our own house. She continued to believe in my father long after I had got tired to waiting.

"We can't live here any more, Anwar," my father said, after the funeral. "You'll need someone to look after you while I'm working."

"Can't I go with you? I can carry the suitcase. I won't disturb you."

"You'll have to start school soon. Best to stay with your mother's folks for the time being. I haven't forgotten about the house in Singapore. I'll get it for you yet. Have faith in me."

My father gave a wink and a winning smile but charm alone was no longer enough for me. I wanted to see him knuckle down to delivering what had been promised, even though my mother could no longer enjoy it.

"I've only seen grandpa and grandma twice," I replied. "I don't know them."

Actually, I was a little afraid of my grandparents. When they touched me during those two visits, their hands felt rough and dry, like the shredded skins of reptiles. My mother's had always been soft and warm and reassuring.

"They'll look after you fine. They're nice people," my father replied, patting me on the head. "I'll come and visit you regularly and send money."

The next day my father packed my few belongings and bought me a slab of my favourite Cadbury's milk chocolate. Then he took me on a four-hour bus journey away from Johore Bahru. The bus snaked through long stretches of rubber plantations, palm groves and lush green countryside and brought us to a small town a couple of miles from the fishing village of my grandparents. We did not reach the small town till well past the lunch hour and we settled for a satay meal at a roadside stall. We then took a trishaw along an unpaved road to our destination.

On arrival, my father had some whispered conversation with my grandfather. I did not hear the words but there seemed to be tension in their murmured exchanges. My father eventually told me to be a good boy till his next visit and left. That was the last I saw of him.

The fishing village was small and secluded. A sparkling sea curled around one side of it and rubber plantations and virgin jungles cradled the other. It consisted of a collection of attap huts, built on stilts and with roofs thatched with leaves of nipah and coconut palms. They were airy and cool, with none of the hemmed-in smells of Johore Bahru.

My grandfather was a wizened, hollow-cheeked man of few words. He had been a clerk in government service but retired to the village to eke out his small pension. The villagers addressed him as "Haji" because he was the only one in the village to have made the pilgrimage to Mecca. Most days he could be seen in his faded sarong, either smoking a long pipe on the verandah of his hut or strolling along the beaches to watch village boats land their catches. Some evenings he would read me passages from the Koran, to the accompaniment of the calls of geckos hunting for insects. The total disappearance of my father did not seem to surprise him but his abandonment of me gnawed me like a poisonous worm.

My grandmother was also wizened and sarong-clad. Instead of smoking, she chewed betel nuts, which stained her uneven teeth with their reddish brown juice. She ran a provision store from the verandah of our hut. The word "store", I came to know later, was an exaggeration because only cigarettes, Lipton's tea and tins of sweetened condensed milk were on offer. The older women of the village gathered there to gossip.

The loving kindness of my grandparents soon put me at ease and soothed my secret disappointments. I consoled myself with the fact that instead of the chaos and foul smells around my former home I now had fresh air, sunshine, clean beaches and murmuring seas. Mangrove roots, rising like cages out of the sea, made ideal playgrounds and the jungles nearby offered wild fruits for the taking. One had to be on guard in the jungles, however, because snakes and wild boars lurked there.

I made friends with other children, in particular with Hamid, a boy a year and a half older than myself, and his sister, Fatima, who was my age. Fatima's smiles and her dark, twinkling eyes reminded me of my mother. Small gangs of us ran around freely, without shirts or shoes, swimming, playing games and hunting for rambutans, mangoes, guavas and breadfruit. When we grappled during games and in mock battles on the beaches I discovered that Fatima's skin also smelt fresh and sweet like my mother's.

My grandmother told me one day that Hamid and Fatima were different because their maternal grandmother was Chinese. She was known in the village as Old Sam. I had seen plenty of Chinese in Johore Bahru but I couldn't tell the difference in the case of Old Sam. The tropical sun had toned her skin into the same colour as ours. She looked just like another old villager in her sarong, chewing betel nuts.

Hamid was expert at climbing coconut trees and, whenever anyone needed a drink, he would scamper up and knock down a couple of fresh green ones. Fatima was very energetic and could run faster than most boys her age. We formed an immediate liking for each other.

Coil of the Serpent

One day, while a group of us was beachcombing, I found the skull of a dog or goat. It had been bleached white by sun and sea and its empty eyes and missing teeth seemed somehow pitiful. I squatted to examine it, not daring to touch it at first. It fascinated me because it had once been part of a living creature. Now its eyes and brains had been eaten by worms. That made me think of my mother. I could not bear the thought that worms might be eating her up at that very moment!

I broke into tears. The other children gathered around and asked what the matter was, but I could not explain.

I took the skull home, not wanting to part with it and yet not knowing what I wanted to do with it. My grandfather merely yawned his disinterest when I showed it to him. My grandmother, on the other hand, immediately ordered me to get rid of it. She said it might bring bad luck. I couldn't understand why. The skull was clean and had no smell. Hamid and I eventually buried it in a patch of jungle.

On our return to the village we found a government education official had turned up. He was a fat man, with a mean mouth and unfriendly eyes. His voice sounded loud and harsh as he berated heads of families for failing to send children to school. Hamid and I were shocked that the bad luck my grandmother had warned about had turned up so soon.

There was nothing we could do about it, however. The next day we put on white shirts and rubber sandals and trudged the two miles to the different schools for boys and girls in the nearest township. We could no longer stay as a group and Fatima and I felt that separation more than the others. The shirt collar scraped against my neck and the sandals did not make for easy walking.

"You should take the opportunity to learn as much as you can," my grandfather said, when I complained about school after the first day. "If you can master English you can land a good job, perhaps a government one in the Straits Settlements. That can bring a pension in your old age."

None of us was interested in jobs or pensions, however. The moment we got home we shed our school clothes and tried to resume our old carefree ways. But somehow things were no longer the same. School had cast a pall over our lives.

One afternoon, about three weeks after school started, I was playing near Fatima's home when her grandmother, Old Sam, caught hold of my arm. "Let me have a look at you," she said, and spun me around to study my back. She let out a cry.

"What's the matter?" I asked.

Instead of answering, Old Sam dragged me back to my grandparent's hut. Fatima, Hamid and the other children followed in noisy procession.

"Look!" Old Sam said to my grandmother, pointing to a spot on my back. "He's been possessed by the Flying Serpent! That cluster is the head of the serpent. If he's not attended to, he'll die. It took the life of a cousin of mine when I was a child."

"What's a Flying Serpent? Where does it come from? Is it contagious?" my grandmother asked, befuddled and alarmed.

"It's a disease known to the Chinese, not contagious," Old Sam replied. "Don't know its origins but Chinese herbalists know how to treat it. Unattended, the serpent will grow. More clusters will appear to encircle his body like a coil. When the clusters have gone round his body, he will die."

I couldn't see what Old Sam was referring to but I could feel my grandmother's rough hand touching a spot on my right shoulder. When I reached for it myself, I felt a small collection of bumps, like hives or insect bites, the size of a large coin. The spot neither hurt nor itched.

"It's nothing," I said, brusquely, not wanting to appear a sissy before the other children. But my heart raced nevertheless when I saw my grandmother turning to my grandfather with a worried look.

"Probably insect bites," my grandfather said, phlegmatically. "Put some Tiger Balm on it."

My companions all wanted to feel the bumps on my shoulder and they did so while my grandmother went to fetch the Tiger

Balm. The balm felt cool and refreshing but all the while I saw Old Sam shaking her head because her advice was being ignored.

"Tiger Balm no good for Flying Serpent," Old Sam muttered.

My grandfather did not take kindly to being contradicted by an old woman. He walked away as if Old Sam's talk of Chinese herbs and a strange disease were no more than the gibbering of a shaman.

I felt nothing unusual for a couple of days. During that time Fatima stuck close to me after school and every now and then ran her fingers over the bumps and asked if I felt any pain. I gave vague replies because I enjoyed her touch.

On the third day, however, I started developing a fever. At the same time, I felt a burning sensation where the head of the Flying Serpent was supposed to be. When the fever climbed the following day and the bumps on my shoulder became more painful, my grandparents took me to a government clinic. The doctor gave me some pills and some ointment.

The medicines were no help. By evening another cluster of bumps appeared on my back, about two inches away from the first. It was slightly smaller in size but just as painful. By morning, a third cluster appeared.

The clusters seemed to follow a diagonal line across my back. I became dazed with fever and pain. My grandmother, now more deeply alarmed, went to fetch Old Sam. The old lady came and shook her head.

"Must get him to a Chinese herbalist," Old Sam urged. "You can see the serpent crossing his back. There's no time to lose. I've made calculations. According to Chinese lunar calendar, Anwar was born in Year of Serpent. The Flying Serpent is very dangerous for such people. In another day or two it will encircle him and it will be too late. Take him now. I can act as interpreter."

My grandparents still hesitated, however. My grandfather thought we should give the medicines from the clinic a chance to work.

The next day I was drifting in and out of consciousness and a fresh cluster rounded my left side. Alarming visions of the skull I had buried flashed across my mind, magnified and seemingly alive.

It took on the appearance of death itself, beckoning me with a hollow and demonic laughter.

During less frightening moments, I was conscious of confused sounds and murmurings. Fragments of agitated consultations between my grandparents and pleas from Fatima entered my brain.

"Please don't die, Anwar. If you do I won't have anyone to play with." Fatima kept whispering close to my ear.

That afternoon my grandparents took me into the township, accompanied by Old Sam. The sole Chinese herbalist practising there prescribed some medicine, which had to be boiled for hours before drinking. He also supplied a muddy reddish paste to be applied to the bumps several times a day.

The boiled medicine tasted foul. But after three days of it, my fever subsided. The reddish paste soothed the pain and brought a comforting sensation of warmth. The clusters gradually retreated, till only the original cluster remained. Within two weeks I was feeling my old self again.

But Old Sam told my grandparents the treatment was not complete.

"The Flying Serpent has not yet been killed," Old Sam said. "It has only been made dormant. It may revive. According to the herbalist, the head must be destroyed, by scorching it with a red-hot poker. That's the only way to prevent a recurrence."

My grandparents, however, baulked at the idea. The original cluster of bumps was allowed to remain undisturbed. Over the years, the bumps faded and protruded less but remained visible. Fortunately, I have never felt the coil of the Flying Serpent again.

It has now been fifty years since my attack and almost forty years since Fatima and I married. I have also served for thirty-five years as a government clerk and earned my pension, just as my grandfather had foreseen. During that time, I have told and re-told my encounter with the Flying Serpent to relatives and friends. They have asked to see and feel the cluster remaining on my right shoulder. Yet none of them had heard of such a disease nor could anyone offer an explanation as to why it should afflict me.

A week ago, however, Fatima and I were asked to dinner by a former colleague whose son had just returned after qualifying as a doctor at Liverpool. My friend invited me to relate my story to his son.

After I had finished, the young doctor said, deferentially, "I haven't much practical experience, Uncle, but it sounds like a case of shingles. Half a century ago, when you had your attack, people didn't know much about viral infections.

"Shingles is basically a viral infection of a nerve. There is a nerve running from the right shoulder round to the front of the belly, along which an infection could manifest itself. Not all the causes of viral attacks have been identified but over-exposure to the sun can be one of them. Once infected, the virus can develop along the path of the nerve, manifest itself in the form of hives and cause a rise in body temperature. In recent years, some new medicines have been developed. There's one called Zovirax. If used early enough, the duration of the infection can be reduced."

"But the herbal medicines I was given seemed to have worked on me," I said.

"Well, that might have been a coincidence. My guess is that the paste you were given contained Capsaicin. That does bring relief to skin pains. On the other hand, there's still a lot we don't know about herbal medicines. Chinese herbalists have been at it for a long time and they might have stumbled onto something. There's a lot of research going on now in Singapore and in Hong Kong."

"Can shingles be life-threatening?" I asked.

"I've never heard so, though I can't rule that out completely. There might be other complications. There's still a lot we don't know about viruses. Normally, when a virus attack is over, the body returns to normal."

"Then how come I still have a cluster of bumps on my right shoulder after fifty years?"

"You've got me there, Uncle!"

It got Fatima too. Every now and then, when I emerge from the shower, Fatima would wonder aloud why the head of the Flying

Serpent remained so stubbornly stamped on my shoulder. I myself give it no mind. I regard it as a happy souvenir, of the days when I was young and almost never lived to remember how wonderful they had been.

An abbreviated version of "Coil of the Serpent" has appeared in the *Evening Standard* in London.

Music From the Past

The blurred frenzy of the lunch hour had subsided when Kung wandered into a McDonald's outlet somewhere between the seedy garishness of Times Square and 54th Street. He had just come away empty-handed from the last of his prospective customers and the futility of his efforts had left him exhausted and hungry.

He had no real expectation of landing orders in New York. His established customers — strung out between Oklahoma and Virginia — had already underscored the depths of the recession. His foray into the Big Apple was merely a desperate attempt to weather the storm

Or was that the whole truth? Ever since he attended Teachers. College at Columbia and met Rachel, every sight and sound of the city seemed to evoke memories of an aching and unconsummated love. Was he merely trying to savour again what had long been lost?

As Kung waited to place his order, he noticed in a corner, on a small dais, a baby grand piano. It seemed altogether out of place in a hamburger eatery. He was not entirely surprised, however, for he had heard of a McDonald's outlet near Wall Street where a tuxedo-clad pianist provided soothing music for harried financial types. He surmised it might be just another franchisee seeking to move up market, though there was no pianist in sight.

His thoughts quickly returned to Columbia and Rachel. He had gone there after national service in Taiwan to learn what he could of Western teaching methods. Rachel was a Jewish girl from the Lower East Side, studying to be a librarian. They had met during one of those welcoming functions for foreign students. They discovered common interests and empathy, which turned rapidly into a singular friendship.

Rachel's dark, Semitic beauty came back to him like an unfulfilled longing. He visualized again her grave brown eyes and the full lips. which needed no adornment by lipstick. Her smiles, too, were heart-breakingly inviting, each one accompanied by a single beguiling dimple playing upon her left cheek.

They were in truth an ill-matched pair. Rachel glowed with rude health and energy whereas he appeared undernourished, preoccupied and desperately in need of womanly care. He gave the impression of someone who ate without regularity and lived too much of life inside his head.

Both of them had clear goals, however. Rachel had her sights on migrating with her parents to Israel whereas he had aimed to run his own school in Taiwan.

He had explained his ambition during the early days of their friendship. "I want one day to run a school like the great academies of the past, perhaps somewhere in the mountains, or at least away from the bustle of city life. I believe that teaching, like great literature, has to have moral content. A teacher has to awaken a spirit of enquiry, to lead those he teaches towards virtue and enlightenment. That has been a tradition in China for over twenty-five centuries, followed by both the Confucians and the Taoists.

"The trouble is that even during their heyday those approaches had deficiencies. The Confucians behaved as if every moral question had already been answered in stone whereas the Taoists were too mystical with their 'teaching without words'. In the West, I suppose the tradition runs back to Socrates. I want to know where the West has reached since."

"You might be in for a disappointment," Rachel replied. "The old verities have gone. The notion of seeking after truth and light is all but defunct, except perhaps in the sciences. It's now largely about ends justifying means. Teaching in New York has less to do with moral issues than with riot control. That's why I stick with books."

During the subsequent years they studied, played and argued together, he slowly realized that differences in race, culture and goals stood like battlements in the way of a closer relationship. He knew his family would look askance at his marrying anyone but a Chinese. Rachel's family undoubtedly would react similarly to her taking up with someone outside her religion and race.

Yet he could not help feeling that in many ways their two races were much alike. Both were prudent, frugal, enterprising, long-suffering and overly burdened by history. They created resentments against themselves by being too clever and successful and by thinking themselves superior to others. What a union between them might produce he was uncertain but he knew in his soul that Rachel was the woman for him. Although she was not overly strict in her religious commitments, formidable obstacles nonetheless remained. The closest he came to broaching his feelings was shortly before graduation, when they were together preparing a kosher Chinese meal.

"I want one day to show you the wonders of China," he said. "But for the present, would Taiwan do? How about paying me a visit after graduation? When I eventually start my school, you can be my librarian."

And she had replied: "Why don't you start a school in Israel? There are enough moral dilemmas there. I'll be glad to be your librarian then."

But he never got to teach, let alone run a school. Shortly after his return to Taipei, his father suffered a stroke and became paralyzed from the neck down. As the eldest son, he had to take over the family business.

His father, a former major in the Kuomintang army, had fled to Taiwan with the remnants of his troops in 1946. There he set up a company to export native products. The military and political stability provided by the United States Seventh Fleet enabled the island to prosper. Exports to America thrived. His mother never lived to enjoy the fruits of that success, however. She died when he was fifteen, leaving behind three sons and three daughters.

His father had a passion for fireworks, developed during his time in the ordnance corps. He established a proprietary brand of firecrackers, rockets, thunder balls and the like under the trade mark of "Red Devil". The products sold exceedingly well in the southern parts of the United States. Although the business handled other products like rattan ware, porcelain and artificial flowers, fireworks were at the core because of high profit margins.

At the insistence of his father he had to master the technical aspects of pyrotechnic mixtures. He learnt that the addition of steel dust could produce a brilliant sparking effect and that a variety of colours could be secured by mixing in lead carbonate or strontium nitrate or cotton fibres. It was all a far cry from metaphysics and teaching methods.

Kung ordered a Big Mac Meal and carried his tray to an empty table. As he settled down to his hamburger, he reflected upon how disagreeable every aspect of the fireworks business had turned out to be. He could not relate to many of the buyers. They seemed over-fed and under-cultivated, sporting massive gold rings, flamboyant shirts, ornate silver belt buckles and snakeskin boots. What he resented most were their over-familiarity, their back-slapping and — because he was young and unsure of himself — their condescending reference to him as "Junior".

His father, though bed-ridden and in need of constant nursing care, nevertheless remained mentally alert. He insisted on keeping up with affairs.

The old man sympathized when Kung reported his antipathies. "I know you have your sights on higher things," his father said. "But the family has to come first. Your brothers and sisters are still young and in need of education. You have completed yours. Someone has to attend to theirs. There is no one else I can turn to."

"You must remember fireworks buyers are not doctors of philosophy. They are rough men in a rough trade. You have to take them as they come. Their demands can sometimes be outrageous but if you look after them, they will return the favour. It's all a matter of you scratching their backs and they scratching yours."

He thought at first that scratching their backs meant dining them royally, showing them the treasures at the National Palace Museum, pampering them at resorts at Sun Moon Lake or, farther afield, introducing them to the scattered ancient temples at Tainan. But he soon realized what they wanted were doctored invoices, kickbacks and the gratification of sexual proclivities.

One day, a buyer from Alabama complained that Red Devil firecrackers were not exploding loudly enough.

"You know there are regulations governing the production of fire-crackers," Kung replied. "A louder report means a more hazardous product. Enough children are being blinded and maimed as it is. The problem is one of irresponsible usage. If it continues, more and more States will ban private discharge of fireworks. Where would you be then? Perhaps you should stop selling to minors."

"Hey, Junior," the Alabama buyer said. "Your old man used to know the score. He knows that guys like me make him rich. Perhaps he hasn't clued you in, so I'll set you straight. Kids back home buy Red Devil because they think they get more bang for the buck. If they don't get the bang, they don't spend the buck. Get it? What people do with stuff after they've bought them is their business. Get my drift, Junior?

When he reported the conversation, his father stated sternly: "Business is like war. You have to exploit the weaknesses of others. You can't have too many scruples. Getting the factory to use a smidge more saltpetre isn't the end of the world, is it? The market is shrinking in any case. One of these days the Mainland is going to crawl out of isolation and undercut us. We must grab the money while we can.

"You must bear three things in mind. First, never skimp on insurance, in case we get landed with product liability suits.

Second, join with others in the trade to hire lobbyists to defend the right to celebrate the Fourth of July with fireworks.

"Third, keep promoting the Red Devil as a distinctive brand. Fireworks are much the same wherever they're produced. But children don't know that. If it can be got across that Red Devil products are in some way superior, children will ask for them. It's all brand identification, like designer labels or trade marks in other businesses."

"Why must we deal in fireworks at all? They injure so many people and start so many fires every year. There are other products we can develop."

"Why shouldn't we sell fireworks, when profits are good? Why should children be deprived of that spice of peril simply because fireworks are capable of being abused? Most things are harmful if improperly handled. Just think of tobacco, alcohol, kitchen knives, matches, weed-killers, sleeping pills, motorcars, anything you like. The list is infinite. If everyone stopped dealing in things capable of being abused, where would the world be?"

After that Kung kept his distaste to himself. His father had set out his duty. He could no more disobey than a foot soldier could a command from a superior. To insist on teaching or starting a school meant turning his back on the family. His conscience denied him any escape.

Every exchange of letters with Rachel reminded him of the mire he was sinking into. Thoughts of going to Israel were as unrealistic as reaching for the moon. The shame of his unresisted bondage gradually killed off their correspondence.

He stuck stoically to his filial duty. But his lack of enthusiasm led to a steady desertion by customers. To prevent his father from discovering the truth, he offered faked profit margins, turnover figures and other misinformation during the bedside briefings.

When profits declined to a level which threatened the well-being of the family and the nursing care required by his father, he swallowed his pride and started wheedling for the return of former customers. He demeaned himself by resorting to the little black book he had inherited, containing telephone numbers of disreputable contacts. He even began putting his signature to documents which could not bear close scrutiny.

He struggled with such distasteful realities for ten years before his father died. With each passing day he came to realize more clearly why tidy aphorisms and neat syllogisms had little place in commercial life. He began to understand too why in ancient times those engaged in commerce were forbidden to enter ancestral temples, lest their presence defiled those sacred places.

After such a long period of lying to his father and being an accessory to knavery, how could he ever take up any pedagogical pursuit? How could he be worthy of a woman like Rachel? He felt consumed by self-disgust.

Worse still, although his father had been dead for five years and he had long since discharged his responsibilities towards his siblings, he nevertheless carried on with the old family trade. Was it sheer inertia and loss of direction? Or was it fear of facing up to how far he had sunk?

Suddenly, through the fog of his self-examination, Kung became aware of the sound of music. He turned and saw a lady at the keyboard of the piano. Her head was covered by a brownish skull cap which hid both the colour and condition of her hair. Her skin, however, was clear and translucent, like that of someone accustomed to a vegetarian diet. He judged her to be older than himself, possibly well advanced in middle age.

She was playing with her eyes closed, with the hint of a smile flirting upon her lips, as if she were performing for some grand audience instead of for just an assortment of munchers of beef patties and French fries.

For a moment Kung speculated whether she had been reduced to providing entertainment during low-budget meals through failure to live up to an earlier promise. He set down his coffee and listened.

As a medley of tunes by Gershwin and Cole Porter filtered through the restaurant, he marvelled at how well the lady played. Gradually, the sentimental quavers carried him back over the years and sensations came drifting back from the wasteland of forsaken dreams.

He was experiencing again quickening summer hopes and sweet winter longings, of Rachel by his side at Broadway shows, in the hushed corridors of the Metropolitan Museum, sampling vegetarian meals in Chinatown, sipping coffee in Village cafes, or walking in Central Park in hazy sunlight after rain. Something more sharp and poignant than grief overwhelmed him. He had allowed the two most important things in his life to slip away, to fizzle out like exhausted Catherine-wheels. In a sudden anguish he wanted to cry out.

When the pianist took a break, he rose to leave. As he passed the old lady, he said: "Thank you for your music. You've brought back a piece of my past."

"I'm glad you like the songs. They're among my favourites," the pianist responded, with a smile. "Were you at one time also a musician?"

"Oh, no," Kung replied, with a bitter laugh. "I was never a musician. I was only a goose — a very silly goose!"

"Music From the Past" has been broadcast by the British Broadcasting Corporation on its World Service and on Radio 4 in Britain.

The Truth About Harry

Stories about Dr. Harry Lee, Fellow of the Royal College of Surgeons and Head of the General Surgical Unit at the Singapore General Hospital, were legion around the hospital and Stephanie Lau had heard most of them. The stories fell into two broad categories — those about the good doctor's surgical skills and those about his turbulent love affairs.

As a scrub nurse who had worked with the doctor for two years, Stephanie could well attest to the accuracy of the surgical stories. She had never seen anyone wield the scalpel with greater authority. Those he had saved could often be seen calling on him, with presents of sweets or fruit as tokens of gratitude.

It was the stories belonging to the latter category that Stephanie had difficulty verifying. That niggled her more than somewhat because she felt she had a right to know. After all, she had been his lover for more than three months.

As Stephanie sat up in her bed, munching a piece of her favourite Swiss chocolate, she tried to tally up the few facts she had culled from the gossip and rumours. About Harry's mesmerising attractiveness there was no doubt. He was tall, dark and of a slim, athletic build. His dark flashing eyes, his head of slightly wavy hair and his sensual mouth with its sardonic smile were frequently the subjects of idle chatter and barely disguised yearnings among nurses. One story had it that his dark complexion came from some distant Malay or Indian ancestor.

Based on her own experience, Stephanie thought Harry's reputation as a philanderer not altogether deserved. It had taken eighteen months of working with him before he dropped his strictly professional attitude and invited her for coffee at the hospital canteen. And that was how it all began.

Stephanie sank her small white teeth into another piece of chocolate. In retrospect she felt somewhat insulted by his reserve. After all, it was not as if she were not a fitting object for his attentions. She was one of the prettiest and brightest nurses in the hospital. Her fresh, open face, framed by a page-boy hair style, and her cheerful disposition made her popular with staff and patients alike.

Her other physical attributes were also stunning. She had a bosom more than ample for a Chinese girl, complemented by a slender waist and taut, rounded haunches, which one admiring intern had described as "the most provocative little arse in all of Singapore."

Though prospective suitors buzzed around her, she remained highly selective. She saw her physical assets as the key to her liberation from the dreary lower middle class existence to which fate had condemned her. They were a treasure to be preserved for the right man and it now occurred to her that the right man might just conceivably be Harry.

The doctor had many of the requirements. He had wealth, status, intelligence and good looks. Moreover, he could make love with a kind of raw animal passion that was at once intoxicating and frightening, that conveyed the sensation of being destroyed by pleasure.

As Mrs. Harry Lee she would not only acquire a high social status but also the power conferred by wealth. That power would compensate her for the hand-me-down clothes of her childhood, the penny-pinching frugality of her adolescence and the cramped and run-down terrace house that passed for home until she moved into the nurses' hostel. It would make possible travel to faraway places, Paris fashions and rare perfumes, sleeping with the feel of silk against her skin and a thousand other extravagances. If only Harry were not so secretive, if only there were not so many question marks over his past, it would be simplicity itself to turn her dreams into reality.

It took quite an effort, for example, to verify something as simple as Harry's marital status. Because of all the rumours, she had taken the opportunity during their first dinner date to remark light-heartedly: "You know, I'm not sure I ought to be seen dining alone with a married man."

"Who says I'm married?"

"Well, some say you married a Scottish girl while studying at the University of Edinburgh. Others say you have a wife in Malaysia."

"You shouldn't listen to gossip," was all that Harry allowed.

Nevertheless she managed to unearth the official facts. Through a friend working in the hospital's personnel department, she sneaked a look at Harry's confidential file. There his marital status was clearly recorded as single and his next of kin was given as his mother, with an address in Malacca. But that information left her only partially satisfied because there remained the disturbing knowledge that much of Harry's notoriety stemmed from the death in unusual circumstances of two women who had been linked romantically to him.

She had clear recollections about the first death, which happened when she was a trainee nurse. It caused a great stir at the hospital. It appeared that Harry had been keeping company with a nurse and the general expectation was that they would marry. Then, suddenly, the nurse was discovered dead from an overdose of sleeping pills. At the inquest Harry testified he had broken off with the girl shortly before her death. The coroner returned a verdict of suicide, when the state of mind of the victim was unbalanced.

Shortly thereafter Harry got engaged to the glamorous but capricious daughter of a Southeast Asian mining tycoon. She had a reputation for high living and pictures of her vacationing in Nice or enjoying the carnival in Rio de Janeiro often graced the pages of regional newspapers. She also had a reputation for speaking her mind. At their engagement party a reporter asked her how she felt about the suicide of the nurse Harry had spurned. She replied she thought Harry worth dying for and declared that if Harry ever abandoned her she would kill herself also. The statement got reported under the headline: "I'll Die For Him Too, Socialite Declares At Engagement Party."

And die she did, a year or so later. She was also found dead from an overdose of sleeping pills. Her body was discovered in the presidential suite of a hotel where she had hosted a fancy dress ball the previous evening. Again Harry testified at the inquest. He admitted having prescribed a sedative for his fiancée's insomnia. Other witnesses testified the deceased had appeared in a jolly mood and had consumed generous amounts of alcohol during the ball. An autopsy confirmed a high level of alcohol in the blood. A verdict of death by misadventure was returned.

Following the inquest, Harry disappeared for a while from the social scene. He spent all his holidays away from Singapore. That led to more rumours and speculations. A story did the rounds suggesting he was heartbroken and on the point of nervous collapse. Other stories, however, suggested he had already found consolation in the arms of another woman. It was around that time that Stephanie was assigned to surgical unit.

Stephanie popped another piece of chocolate into her mouth and licked her thumb and forefinger voluptuously. The more she thought about Harry the more she realized how very little she knew about him. Although Harry was a marvelous raconteur, none of the stories he told revealed very much about himself. Even when he invited her to his home, he seemed reluctant to admit her to more than a small part of his bungalow at a time. Stephanie could not help laughing in recalling the excruciatingly long time it took to gain access to his bedroom.

Harry's bungalow was located in an exclusive district. During her first visit she did not manage to penetrate beyond the sitting room, where they drank, chatted and listened to Mozart.

"Don't you think his music marvellous?" Stephanie had asked, as they listened to Serenade in G. "There's so much feeling and emotional depth."

"It's really the early flowering of Mozart's genius that I find intriguing," Harry had replied. "Fancy mastering the harpsichord by the age of three and composing symphonies by ten! Can you imagine what the world could be like if we could breed such people? I have my own theories about genetic engineering. One of these days I'm going to test them."

Stephanie did not manage to get beyond the sitting room on her second visit either, although she did manage to study more closely the various paintings and lithographs decorating the walls. Since her grasp of art was such that she could not tell the difference between a Picasso and a Pissarro, she had no idea of their merits or shortcomings. Most of them appeared to be colourful and pleasant, except for one with sombre figures. The figures both fascinated and unsettled her. They caused her to observe: "Isn't that a rather depressing picture to have in a sitting room?"

"It's quite something, isn't it?" Harry replied.

"Who are those people and who is the artist?"

"That is a rather fine reproduction of van Gogh's The Potato Eaters."

"Van Gogh? Wasn't he supposed to be mad?"

"Yes, I suppose he was. But then, most exceptional people are, aren't they?"

That question left Stephanie somewhat at a loss, so she merely mumbled a reply. In truth she had never met anyone whom she considered exceptional. She had been taught at school that people like Einstein, Gandhi and Confucius were exceptional. But her teachers never mentioned anything about their being mad.

On her third visit she gained access to the kitchen. Harry had offered to cook her a curry dinner and she had insisted on helping. It turned out to be one of the best curries she ever had.

On her fourth visit she was introduced to the library, which was located in a room permanently air-conditioned to keep out the tropical damp. She had never seen so many books in a private home before. There were, of course, the standard medical books like Gray's Anatomy and the set of six manuals by Cunningham. But the rest were unfamiliar to her. Their authors had strange foreign names like Dostoyevsky, Loti, Poe, de Sade, Nietzsche and Baudelaire. Many others appeared to deal with uncommon subjects like theories of natural selection, the life of the Borgias or the Spanish civil war.

She searched among the volumes for her own favourite book, Gone With The Wind, but could not find it. She could not understand how anyone with so many books could be without Gone With The Wind.

She made it to the bedroom only on her seventh visit.

Stephanie reached out for another piece of chocolate, hesitated, then closed the box with resolution, conscious of the damage already done to her figure. It occurred to her maintaining a relationship with Harry was like eating chocolates. It was delicious and enjoyable, so long as one did not worry about the calories in such tasty morsels. But, unfortunately, she could not help worrying about the mysteries surrounding Harry.

Only the previous evening, as she lay in his arms after a frantic bout of lovemaking, she had complained good-naturedly: "You know, I really know next to nothing about you."

"I love you. What else is there to know?" Harry relied.

"Well, a girl usually wants to know things about the man she loves. She wants to know about the things he likes or dislikes, what he did before they met, what his old flames were like, and things like that."

"I enjoy books which deal seriously with their subjects, I enjoy curries, and I prize privacy. I choose friendships sparingly and I loathe idle gossip and other mindless ways of wasting time. Before I met you I studied medicine and then I practised it. As for old flames, I can tell you nothing. My past belongs to those who have shared it with me, just as your past belongs to those who have shared it with you. By the same token, the present belongs to both of us and to nobody else. Relationships are not meant to be recounted like casual tales."

How strange Harry was, Stephanie thought, as she recalled the conversation. He was deep where other men were shallow. She only wished she could plumb those depths. Maybe he would be less of a mystery if she read some of the books he read. The thought came like a revelation. Yes, why had she not thought of it before? She would attack that great library of his at the first opportunity, she determined, as she prepared for bed.

On her next visit to Harry's home, she made a point of browsing in the library. But she hardly knew where to begin. At last she selected a volume handsomely bound in tooled morocco entitled Love, in the expectation that its contents would illuminate something dear to her own heart.

"May I borrow this?" Stephanie asked, holding up the book for Harry to see.

"Ah, Stendhal!" Harry said, with a genuine note of pleasure in his voice. "He was the man who identified the Salzburg phenomenon. No doubt you are aware of it."

"Yes, but I didn't realize it originated with Stendhal," Stephenie lied.

"I hope you enjoy the book. But take good care of it. It is a rather special volume."

"Oh, I will," Stephanie promised.

When Stephanie got home, she ran a hot bath in preparation for sleep. It was one of the few luxuries she could enjoy at the hostel. She was also anxious to discover what the Salzburg phenomenon was, for she hated to appear ignorant. So she took Stendhal to read while soaking in the bath. But the bath was so deliciously soporific and Stendhal so incredibly dull that she soon fell asleep.

When she woke up with a start, she found pages of Stendhal floating in the tepid water and the tooled morocco cover with the remainder of the book resting upon her body in a soggy mess.

The week that followed was one of sheer agony. She dashed around bookshops all over the city for a replacement copy. But nothing approaching tooled leather could be had. All she could find was a copy in the paperback Penguin Classics.

During that week, her meetings with Harry were filled with unease. Harry quickly sensed something was amiss. So she confessed her accident in a sobbing voice.

Harry's reaction seemed rather odd. He expressed neither anger nor surprise. He did not console her or offer forgiveness either. Instead, he kept repeating in a flat, abstracted voice: "You dropped my Stendhal in the bath. You dropped my Stendhal in the bath." It was as if he could not believe his ears.

Following that disaster, Stephanie could not find it in herself to ask Harry for the loan of another book. Instead, she noted a few likely titles and purchased her own copies. But most of them proved less than readable. Certainly none of them was anywhere as absorbing as Gone With The Wind.

While she continued to struggle with those impossible volumes, she continued to see Harry. Although things appeared normal on the surface, she detected subtle alterations in their relationship. Their eyes did not seem to meet in the operating theatre as frequently as before and when they did meet she could no longer read in them unambiguous messages of love. Their evenings together were often cut short on one pretext or another.

Such developments filled Stephanie with alarm. She knew with all the certainty of feminine intuition that if she did not remedy the situation she would lose Harry. Desperate situations called for desperate measures, she told herself. So that evening, after they had made love, she seized the bull by the horns.

"Darling, why don't we get married?" she said.

"That's a big step," Harry said.

"We love each other, don't we? It's only logical that people who are in love should marry."

"What passes for love is often no more than a simple rush of body fluids to the groin. Once that condition has been corrected the world takes on a different hue. I am not the easiest man in the world to live with. It would be wise to wait a bit."

As Stephanie listened, a terrible chill entered her heart. The message was unmistakable. Harry was drifting away. Panic seized her. Something dramatic had to be done to save the situation. She remembered the sleeping pills Harry sometimes used, which he kept in the drawer of his bedside table. There was already a glass of water on the table. So she took out the bottle, poured the little white pills onto the bed and began swallowing them two or three at a time.

Harry was a doctor, she calculated, as she swallowed. It was his job to save lives. She had watched him do so with consummate skill day in and day out. If she took an overdose, he would be forced to take her to the hospital to pump out her stomach. It would not be a pleasant experience but it would create a scandal. Harry, with his shaky reputation, could hardly risk further opprobrium if marriage offered an easy way out. There seemed no flaw in her logic.

"What in heaven's name are you doing?" Harry asked, looking at her sternly.

Stephanie did not reply but continued to swallow the pills. After taking about forty pills, she mustered all the emotion she could and said: "I love you, Harry, and I don't want to live without you."

"It's a damn fool thing to do," Harry said, still staring sternly at her.

The remonstration sounded almost like an endearment and Stephanie smiled. "I want you to be happy, Harry," she said, remembering how one of her favourite movie actresses had uttered a similar line. "If I cannot make you happy, I don't want to be in your way."

Stephanie saw Harry shake his head. He then got out of bed and began dressing. Things were developing as she had foreseen, she thought. She was starting to feel drowsy and short of breath. She allowed the drowsiness to wash over her, confident that at any moment Harry would gather her up and head for the hospital.

After Harry had dressed, he came to her side of the bed and bent over her. Stephanie got the impression he was examining her pupils. She smiled at him. "Before I die, please tell me that you do love me a little," she said in a slurred voice. That line, too, had been retrieved from some movie she had seen.

Harry straightened himself and stood looking at her for what seemed like an eternity. "Love you? I have longed to love a woman who could bear me children like Mozart. Do you imagine that can be achieved by someone so frivolous as to drop Stendhal in the bath?" The mockery in his voice was undisguised.

Stephanie struggled through a haze to grasp what Harry had said. Then she saw Harry walking away. She tried to cry out but her throat would only emit a rasping sound.

At the door, Harry paused to turn to look at her again before closing the door silently behind him. She wanted to get up, to get help, but could not move. She was seized by unmitigated terror and during that one eternal moment before oblivion she finally discovered the truth about Harry.

"The Truth About Harry" has appeared in *The Peak* magazine in Hong Kong.

Slow Poisons

"Why keep playing the romantic? Marriage's no big deal. Studio thinks it'll boost my career. Who am I to argue? Love's got nothing to do with it."

"Then why not marry me? You say you love me. Why marry that idiot William Tung?"

"Must we go into that again? You're a Yank, darling. My fans won't wear it."

"Yes, I know! I'm a gweilo, a barbarian, beneath contempt! But I can't see that William Tung's any catch. He's a womanizer. He'll dump you the moment he finds a new toy. The only thing that's going for him is a very rich father who's conveniently very dead."

"I know what he is. But he's socially prominent. He's chairman of the General Chamber of Commerce. He's got the clout to get me into the right circles. He can give me everything I want — cars, furs, apartments, bank deposits in safe places. It's a business transaction, pure and simple. There's nothing to stop us from continuing as we are."

Dick Stanton recalled the most recent of his arguments with Apricot as he poured himself a generous helping of scotch. As he added ice, he recalled also the wounding remark he had checked on the tip of his tongue.

Could this be the final straw, he wondered. Would he stoop to adultery for the sake of an unravelling affair? He rose wearily from the wicker chair with his drink, rested his elbows on the balcony railing and pressed the chilled glass against his broad, furrowed brow. His deep-set eyes, profound and unquiet, brimmed with misery. The sound of Bach's Fugue in E Flat floated out from the sitting room behind.

Not a good night for Bach, he reflected. His mind was not following the chasings. It was darting about like some startled dragonfly amidst the broiling chaos of his life. The partnership offer from Mega Communications was a distraction he did not need.

Stanton was dressed only in a pair of blue pajama trousers and he seemed insensitive to the coolness of the cement floor beneath his bare feet. His torso, with its pale mat of curls, was no longer lean and well-defined as it used to be when he was a sprinter on the Stanford track and field team. Rich foods and alcohol, as much as the passage of years, had added accretions of flesh.

He took a long draught from his glass. Good old Johnnie Walker, he thought, the only friend a man could share his troubles with. He allowed his eyes to roam over the brooding granite hills lying to the north. The moon hung like a discoloured lemon drop upon a sombre sky. Beneath the hills, known as the Nine Dragons, the lights of the city beckoned like a mirage.

How captivating, he thought. So pretty and enticing. One speck was indistinguishable from another, yet together they formed a veritable fairyland. No wonder tourists enthused over them in letters and postcards home. They must stir up pleasurable memories of shopping orgies, exotic feasts and, for the daring, nocturnal depravities undreamt of in Ames, Iowa, or Painesville, Ohio.

Apricot was every bit as captivating as those lights. She was, after all, skilled in the arts of fantasy and make-believe. The pouting playfulness of her lips, the candid promises in her eyes, the savage voluptuousness of her breasts, all constituted the stuff of dreams. Every aspect of her person had been worshipped, pored over and lusted after by viewers of bad Cantonese movies and subscribers to certain types of magazines. Small wonder her studio had insured her bust with Lloyd's of London for untold millions.

But, like the lights of the city, she had an underside. He had reminded himself a thousand times she was a confused, exploited woman, driven by warped ambitions. She was not the kind of woman to inspire heroes or to sustain those with lofty dreams. Yet, even if she embodied all the corruption, all faithlessness in the world, he still could not stop wanting her.

Before meeting her, his life had been focused. He had literary aspirations. An impulse throbbed in his veins. He wanted to master Flaubert's mot juste and capture Kipling's "magic of the necessary word." He sought, like Conrad, to move the world with his art.

While earlier generations of Americans turned to Europe, he had chosen Asia. The reasons were tangled. A childhood in San Francisco, close to Chinatown. The flower children norms of the Sixties absorbed during his teens. His father's grievous wounds, sustained during the battle for Okinawa, and the death twenty years later of his elder brother in the jungles of Vietnam. They all nurtured a desire to know Asia, to discover whether its ancient civilizations could explain the perplexities of his age.

After graduating from Stanford with a degree in English he bade farewell to his parents and set out with backpack and good intentions, to marinate in the cultural juices of the East. He began by spending two years in Japan, absorbing what he could of Zen and Shinto. Then followed a similar stint in Taiwan, observing a society still imbued with the precepts of Confucius and Mencius.

He lived in flop houses or slept rough when weather permitted. He earned his keep by teaching English. It was a comfortless existence but he did not mind. His concern was to reach understandings he could fashion into art.

He had arrived in Hong Kong on transit to Southeast Asia. The city arrested him. The press of people was intolerable, the noise deafening, the pace of life vertiginous. A boastful vitality seemed to bounce off its congested pavements and ricochet around its towering buildings. The place struck him like a cocky, mongrel metropolis where the sadistically modern went hand in hand with the most primitive of superstitions.

The place reeked of wealth. Its economy was the envy of the world. It boasted full employment, bulging reserves, painlessly low taxes and consistent surpluses. All day long and well into the night pile drivers, jack hammers, pneumatic drills, sweating labourers and chanting coolies toiled on fresh monuments to capitalism. But beneath the institutionalised rituals and the surface obsequiousness there lurked an unavowed Eastern resentment against Western intrusions.

In order to get to the heart of the phenomenon, he decided to tarry a while. He had his hair cut to slough off his hippie image and took on a poorly paid job as reporter with one of the English language newspapers, the Morning Standard. After eighteen months of bewildering experiences, he met Apricot.

She was then a moody seventeen-year-old, working as a waitress in a cheap cafe. He had gone for a cup of coffee and noticed at once the feline provocativeness in her eyes. In spite of her ill-fitting uniform, he could also discern the weighty voluptuousness of her breasts and the sensual promises of her hips.

When she came to serve, she accidentally spilt some coffee on him. He let out a yell, although the scalding was not serious. She immediately became flustered. In order to calm her, he said: "How about discussing damages after work?"

He had meant it as a mild flirtation but to his surprise she responded quickly: "Okay. Okay. I get off at seven."

He waited outside the cafe at the appropriate time, puzzled and expectant. When she emerged, she was palpably tense. Her first words were: "I can't pay money. Please don't make me lose job."

"Hey! Relax! I'm not after anything. Just being friendly."

"You wanted damages. That means you're after something."

"Look, let's forget this. I just thought it might be nice to get to know you."

"Why?"

"Don't know. You're an attractive girl working in a crummy cafe. I'm a reporter with the Morning Standard. There must be a human interest angle somewhere. Where does a girl like you come from? Why are you not in school? Why can't you do something better than wait on tables in such a dump? What do you want out of life? What are your hopes, your dreams? That's the sort of stuff I'm after."

The wariness in her eyes softened at the mention of a newspaper. "You're really reporter?"

"Sure," he said, producing his press pass and recognizing at the same time her potential for beauty. In spite of her moodiness and ill-fitting clothes, he judged her a raw, green bud whose loveliness and fragrance had yet to unfold.

"You can get me into films?"

He almost laughed at the banality of her request. "Let's talk about it over a drink," he replied.

Her story was depressingly familiar. A dead father at the age of twelve, a school drop-out at fourteen, and thereafter the mainstay of a family consisting a mother and four younger brothers and sisters. Home was a one-room cubbyhole at the Shek Kip Mei resettlement estate.

Shek Kip Mei had once been the site of a massive squatter settlement. A horrendous fire levelled it. Upon its ruins a cheerless government estate had arisen. He had been there in the course of his assignments. The graffiti on its walls, the young louts lounging along its grubby corridors, the Peeping Toms lurking outside its communal latrines and bathrooms, were standard fixtures. It was an urban jungle.

As she unfolded her story, he noticed she fidgeted with her left thumb, the nail of which had been well chewed. He also noted a restlessness in her eyes, as if they had to be on constant alert. He put that down to the uncongenial life at Shek Kip Mei.

He was at that point ready to move on. Hong Kong, with its endless incongruities, fascinated him still. He had filled a dozen notebooks with jottings and plots. Ideas for stories were beginning to intrude upon him. He did not want to be sidetracked.

But something about Apricot appealed to his sense of compassion. Her potential for beauty beckoned him like a challenge. He felt an inexplicable urge to fashion a creature of grace and beauty out of that unappreciated lump of human clay. He might even create a woman embodying his most cherished ideals.

He had little money for the endeavour. But his journalistic work had given him wide connections and a store of favours due. He brought them into play, securing for Apricot lessons in elocution, deportment and make-up. He told her that mastery of those skills was a prerequisite for a film career. He himself saw to the fluency and idiomatic enrichment of her English.

Apricot was a fast learner. Within months her appearance and disposition became transformed. She grew more vivacious and less moody and fidgeted less with her thumb. She not only began to draw admiring glances in the streets but became the frequent object of salacious remarks at her place of work.

He wanted to settle her in more suitable employment before moving on, possibly as a salesgirl at one of the smarter department stores. But her heart was set on films. He did not believe she had talent and was fearful for her in that shallow and money-driven calling, with its misama of corruption and underworld entanglements.

But her sheer persistence cajoled him into securing her a screen test at one of the less well-established film studios. Even as he arranged it, he hoped it would turn out badly. Unfortunately, it proved a success and Apricot was offered a bit part, with three words of dialogue. She became so ecstatic that in the afterglow of that quite insignificant achievement they became lovers.

Stanton emptied his glass and replenished it, recalling with a helpless longing the delicious feel of her skin and the bountifulness of her breasts, so often proffered like overflowing wineskins. The remembered explorations with lips and tongue still set him afire.

Apricot's acting debut whetted her appetite. Her head bubbled with crazy enthusiasms. She wanted to dress fashionably and be noticed in high society. That required more money and connections than either of them had. The odd invitation might be winkled out from newspaper contacts but glamorous clothing and accessories were beyond the wages of a mere reporter.

Apricot was so determined to get her way, however, that she was ready to resort to loan sharks. He knew where that would lead. Perhaps he should have abandoned her there and then. But he felt responsible. When he failed to deflect her, compassion and decency demanded that he find the funds. That meant taking up more lucrative employment. So he resigned from the Morning Standard and, against his better judgement, joined a celebrated advertising firm.

He reconciled himself to the shifty art of singing the praises of detergents, sanitary napkins, instant noodles and other pedestrian products at Mega Communications. In spite of his contempt for such work, his efforts caught the eye of Sol Zimmermann, the head of the firm and a fellow American.

"Hey, you're a wizard with words," Zimmermann declared, on examining the results of his first assignment. "I bet you can sell manure in paradise, if you set your mind to it."

What followed was a three-year contract, complete with a modest furnished apartment a third of the way up Victoria Peak. It was the first presentable home he could call his own. After adding a few decorative touches, he invited Apricot to share it. She accepted. After all, Shek Kip Mei was hardly a commendable address for an aspiring actress.

During their time together he tried to advance her spiritually and intellectually. He told her tales from the great books and explained the fundamentals of art. He tried to interest her in Western music. But she had no taste for either Beethoven or Bach. For her, the movie extravaganza represented the acme of Western culture.

Notwithstanding the intellectual gulf that lay between them, the pleasures of the flesh soon had him hopelessly in love. One evening, during one of those unguarded moments after love, he told Apricot of his desire to become a writer.

"Are you going to write books that sell a zillion and make you filthy rich?" Apricot asked, brightly.

"Afraid not," he replied. "That's for entertainers. I want to write about deeper truths. Humans have been described as formidable beasts of prey, for we are the only creatures preying systematically on our own kind. Yet we remain capable of love, courage, compassion and nobility. What makes us that way? I want to explore that. Unfortunately, that kind of stuff doesn't sell."

"I shouldn't wonder! Who wants the nastiness in themselves to be dug up and exposed to the world? Why not concentrate on what makes people feel good? Then you'll be rich and successful. Isn't that the American dream?"

"Being rich and being successful do not always go together, at least not for writers. A writer may become rich because people buy his books but that does not mean he is successful. The test of success is whether his ideas remain relevant a thousand years after he's gone. So writers never know whether they have been successful. That is a judgment for posterity."

"You must be a crazy romantic! In this town everybody knows success means money and money means success. It's as simple as that."

"Ah! That's why this town is filled with more rich failures than any other place I know. Beyond a certain point money is an encumbrance upon the soul."

"That's easy to say for people who've never been without! For me, I want money, lots of it. I want to be able to smell it, taste it and run my fingers through it. I don't care what happens after I'm dead."

He made no attempt to argue further. He figured her for an intelligent girl who, given time and proper tutelage, could be led towards loftier ideals. He was prepared to bide his time.

One day, Apricot returned home in a state of high excitement, declaring she had been signed for a starring role. The script she produced was laughable. Its storyline was almost non-existent. It was about a girl searching for love but finding herself taken advantage of at every turn. It was little more than an excuse for romping around bedrooms in various stages of undress.

His heart sank. He could well imagine the abomination such a script would produce. But it proved impossible to deflect Apricot.

When he subsequently attended the preview, he felt an inexpressible sense of betrayal. The images of Apricot simulating the act of love on the screen were painfully realistic. It was as if everything pure and precious between them had been desecrated.

The film's sizzling love scenes created a sensation and Apricot's reputation as a sex kitten was launched. She found herself a manager and offers flooded in, together with demands for photographic features from magazines.

He viewed such projects with mounting distress. When she eventually decided to pose in the nude, he lost his temper. "Why do you keep doing this kind of trash?" he demanded.

"Why are you upset? Brigette Bardot made money doing it, why shouldn't I?" Apricot replied.

"Because I love you. Why should you allow pimply kids and dirty old men to snigger over your nakedness? Besides, Brigette Bardot never went so far. Where is the art in what you're doing? It's puerile. You might as well go the whole hog and make blue movies."

"I thought you were an open-minded person. I'm just doing what my manger tells me, to bring in money."

"Money? Is that what this is all about? Showing off your body for money?"

"My body is all I've got. Let's face it, I'm never going to be the great actress you wish me to be. I'm never going to play Lady Macbeth or Camille. So why shouldn't I use what I've got?"

"I don't understand you. Don't you care how I feel or how your family might feel? Don't you have any shame or self-respect? Why debase yourself like some cheap whore?"

"My family understands me. It's a pity you don't! What kind of self-respect does anybody learn in Shek Kip Mei? It's hard enough simply to survive. I've lived worse than any whore, if you must know. Do you know how many times I've been beaten and gang-raped? I've had to grit my teeth and bear it. Since everybody likes my body, why shouldn't I get something out of it too?"

Apricot stopped abruptly, convulsed with sobs. Tears gushed from her eyes and she brushed them away fiercely, almost defiantly, with the back of a hand.

The revelation stunned him into silence. All of a sudden she appeared pitiful and child-like, vulnerable and in need of succour. He rushed to embrace her, holding her tightly and stroking her hair, whispering the while: "Hush, hush, sweetheart. Don't cry. Don't cry. Nobody is ever going to hurt you again. I'll see to it. I'll protect you from now on."

Stanton emptied his glass and returned to his wicker chair. He sat down wearily. Bach had been replaced by the murmur of the traffic, floating up steadily from the road below. As he poured another drink he noted that the bottle was half gone. He was not doing too badly, he thought, for a bottle-a-night man.

For weeks after that traumatic evening, he wrestled with Apricot's suffering. He could visualize the terror-filled eternities in dark places, the blows, the blood, the stifled screams, the carnal barbarities. He was a stranger to such horrors. He had never existed at the margins, poised upon the narrow edge between life and death as his father and brother had been. How could he possibly apprehend what Apricot had to endure? He was amazed she had coped with so much.

Could her displays of nakedness now represent a cry of triumph or an act of defiance, to taunt those who could no longer take their pleasure from her? Or was it a kind of self-therapy, to purify her humiliations? Or had she gone beyond that, to a point where nothing meant anything any more? He wished he knew enough about the human mind to probe into its dark byways.

He could not help blaming himself for her plight. A vain impulse had caused him to intervene in her life, little realizing she had no defence against the world except her will to survive. He had pitched her headlong into the most obnoxious end of that over-heated and manipulative world of films. She was bound to be exploited as she had been in Shek Kip Mei. Looking ahead, what could be in store except a neurotic, suicidal and drug-spangled finale?

From the moment of their first kiss, their first embrace, a part of himself had been surrendered. He came to need her as much as air. He had no alternative but to stay and attempt to wean her from the life she had chosen. So he signed up for another three years with Mega Communications.

For a while Apricot appeared genuinely torn between continuing with her career and fear of his disapproval. She declined some offers and prevaricated on others. But that brought a return of her moodiness and the gnawing upon her thumbnail began again.

Realizing the loss of income would affect Apricot's family, he offered to step into the breach. But Apricot refused. Her family was her responsibility, she declared. It wanted no charity.

After a period of impasse, he reluctantly acquiesced in her returning to work. Her temporary retreat apparently did her career no harm. Quite the contrary. The powers-that-be thought she was holding out for more and some quite ludicrously large offers resulted. But the scripts remained pathetically devoid of artistic merit.

Increasing income enabled Apricot to move her family out of Shek Kip Mei. She introduced him to her folks and he welcomed their periodic visits. The mother was a dull, illiterate woman, but eminently likeable. Unlike most Chinese mother's, she did not seem bothered by her daughter's involvement with a gweilo.

Apricot's brothers and sisters obviously relished their changed circumstances. They held him in awe, assuming that his power and connections as a gweilo had been responsible for advancing their sister's circumstances.

Gradually, as Apricot acquired star status, her time became no longer her own. She was perpetually on the move, with shooting schedules, rehearsals, conferences, hairdressers, photographic sessions, physical work-outs and public appearances. She stayed out late, socializing and pandering to the hysteria of her fans, and returned too exhausted for anything but sleep. He felt increasingly lonely and restless and turned to Johnnie Walker for relief.

Such an existence in limbo might have remained tolerable for a good while, except for an unexpected revelation. Late one night, Apricot returned in high spirits and much the worst for drink. Before she passed out, she blurted out triumphantly that a big producer had signed her to star in three films with enormous budgets.

As he undressed her to put her to bed, he noticed upon her breasts and her buttocks love bites not of his making. Then, mingling with the fumes of alcohol, he detected the spoor of love-making. It devastated him to discover how Apricot had been advancing her career!

In matters of the heart, the stronger had to make concessions to the weaker, he argued with himself. Fate had dealt the girl a rotten hand. She had suffered enough, endured enough. What good would recriminations do? They would merely erode whatever remained of her self-esteem. He was supposed to be an intellectual, an idealist, a decent human being. Wasn't he large enough to overlook an inebriated lapse or two? After all, fidelity was not the only virtue. Had he not pledged his honour to protect and care for her?

The only way to discharge his obligations was to remove her from the financial blandishments of her calling. That meant getting her away from Hong Kong. So he proposed marriage.

He spoke of the life they could have in America, drawing delightful word pictures of California and San Francisco, of scenic Monterey and the forests of the Sierra Nevada, of wide open spaces and limitless opportunities. He even argued the sheer commonsense of getting settled elsewhere before the Communists came in 1997.

"Oh, darling, I would love nothing better than to marry you," Apricot replied.

"But I can't. At least, not yet. I'm just beginning to make a name. If I'm to make it big, it has to be now, before the Commies come. Can you imagine Red Flag running me as a centrefold? I have the chance to make enough to take care of my family. Can't throw that away. A few more years. Please, darling."

"This is no way to live," he countered. "I hardly see you and when you get home you are too tired for anything but sleep."

"I know it's a trial, darling, but it'll be over soon. Three years at the outside, I promise. Then we can marry and raise a family. I'll do whatever you want. But please, don't make me give up now."

"And what am I suppose to do for the next three years?"

"You've got a good job at Mega. I'm sure Sol will offer you a partnership before long."

"I know he will, but working for Mega is not a job. It's an enslavement. Don't you realize I'm nothing more than a corporate pimp on an expense account? I want to get stuck into my writing. I'm already thirty-six and I haven't published a damn sentence, except for all that advertising crap."

"Then why don't you quit? Go do your thing. I can support you. I can afford it now."

"That's kind of you but that's not the point. I can't write here. I need breathing space. There are too many distractions. The noise, the debaucheries, the claustrophobia, the chromium-plated pretences, the hothouse atmosphere. The city is just a bit of counterfeit China designed for counterfeit lives."

"Then go to one of the outlying islands."

"Yes, and when will we ever see each other? I need to be with you, don't you understand? Are you going to visit me once a month, as if I were serving time in Alcatraz?"

The questions hung unanswered in the air. There seemed no way out. She was too wrapped up with her own ambitions and he was enslaved by a love which defied every abasement, every wounding of the heart. To each a different poison, he thought.

Stanton's introspections were interrupted by the full-throttled roar of a powerful sports car racing up the hill. The noise changed timbre as the vehicle charged along the serpentine road, before receding into the distance. Some wealthy failure enjoying the vulgar thrill of speed, he surmised. For a moment he envied its driver. He was probably racing along without a care, a stranger to any interrogation of the soul.

Stanton glanced up at the moon. It seemed to frown with disgust over his recurring angst and his whiskey-sodden self-pity. He had failed one opportunity after another to bring an end to the affair. He could have disengaged honourably when Apricot's manager pressed her to move into a flat of her own or when Apricot began the public charade of being squired around by rich or decorative Chinese bachelors. But he had accepted those impositions without demur.

Although Apricot left him the keys to her flat and had given him carte blanche to drop by whenever he chose, he had stayed away. He was fearful of what he might stumble into. So he simply sat and waited for her, with a sad, sick longing, and drank himself into unrefreshing slumber night after night. When she did come, their love-making was no longer as before. It became as if each was trying to fake an ardour that was already slipping away.

He could not rid his imagination of the fat producers, handsome actors and rich playboys invading her arms and her bed. He lost all urge to write. Neither could he muster the concentration to read. He began doubting if he ever had an authentic gift.

The day after Apricot had announced her marriage plans, he screwed up the will to tell Sol Zimmermann he wanted to leave.

Zimmermann was beside himself. "Hey, you're not going solo on me, are you? You haven't landed a contract with your filly's studio after all these years, have you?"

"No, Sol. It's just that I've had enough of this place. I want to go home, to get back to some serious writing."

"Hey, baby, there ain't nothing more serious than what you're doing. It's big bucks. Don't throw it away. Forget that literary crap. That's for masochists. Okay, maybe you've been under pressure. The workload has been unbelievable. The word doing the rounds is that Apricot has split but there're plenty of chicks around. Just don't talk of scat-doodling home. I'll tell you what, let's talk partnership. I can't be whiter than that, can I? Gimme a week and I'll get a package to you. Don't say anything now. We can talk when you've studied the deal."

Sol Zimmermann was as good as his word. A draft contract was delivered five days later. But Stanton tossed it unread onto his coffee table.

Stanton emptied his glass again. He had at last arrived at what a fellow American had once described as the moment of truth. No matter how much he loved Apricot or how culpable he felt over her predicament, he knew he could no more save her than he could save rain forests or endangered species.

The only remaining question was whether he could save himself. His youth had slipped away. Middle age waited around the corner. He recalled vaguely Lawrence saying something about people shedding their sicknesses through books. Was that a possibility? Conrad did not publish his first novel till he was thirty-eight. Shaw never wrote anything amounting to a row of beans till after forty. Tolstoy did some of his best stuff in his dotage. Perhaps there was hope for him yet.

Stanton picked up the bottle to pour himself another drink and noted with surprise that three fingers of whiskey remained. He did not need to be a bottle-a-night man after all, he thought, as he set the bottle down again with a thump.

He rose unsteadily to his feet. This was always the most difficult part, he reminded himself, getting to the bathroom and then to bed without knocking over too many things. As he faltered through the sitting room, he saw the draft contract from Mega Communications on the coffee table.

He allowed himself a smile. Tomorrow he would tell Sol Zimmermann to stick it up his fundament.

Night Ferry From Macau

It was 4.00 a.m. when the aged ferry shuddered under way. As usual on a Monday, it was filled to capacity, its pre-dawn departure being particularly suitable for gamblers extending their weekend sprees in Macau. The three-and-a-half-hour journey from the ancient Portuguese enclave to the British Colony of Hong Kong provided just sufficient time for a good nap before resuming the quotidian struggle for a more moneyed existence.

But a nap was out of the question for Pao, standing listlessly upon the after deck. Others could sleep. His burly escort could sleep. He was left mulling the consequences of having gambled and lost. Yet, oddly, he felt neither apprehension nor regret, only a strange sense of inevitability. It amused him to think that he had finally come up with a formula for turning adversity to advantage!

The night was dark and portentous, the deck crowded with shadows. The windows of the second-class cabins, steamed up by the slumbering hordes within, threw only a grudging light upon the throbbing darkness of the deck. Pao's features, therefore, remained obscured.

Otherwise, an observer might have discerned a thin, middle-aged man with an angular physiognomy. His complexion was sallow and washed out, suggestive of a lack of sleep. The forehead was indented at the temples, with high cheekbones shearing into hollow cheeks. Two vertical frown lines marked the space between nondescript eyebrows. A half-smoked cigarette dangled from a thin, sullen mouth. The small hands resting upon the deck failing were unremarkable, save for a missing little finger on the left hand.

Pao had not always looked that way. There had been a time when his features were attractively rounded and cushioned, when his eyes shone with intelligence. But that was before defeats and humiliations turned him into a stranger to hope.

The sea breeze, still edged by spring chill, caused Pao to shiver momentarily. He turned up the collar of his gabardine jacket, which still retained a certain faded smartness. He spat out the remainder of his cigarette and watched its frail speck disappear into the undifferentiated darkness merging sea and sky.

It occurred to him he had wasted more than half his life chasing the favours of the Goddess of Chance. Gambling seemed a peculiarly Chinese disease. Perhaps its germ had been planted among his people too early, during the traditional festivities marking each Lunar New Year.

He recalled the exploding fireworks, the resounding felicitations and, most of all, the red *lai-see* packages containing money handed out by adults. As a child he had longed to spend those bounties on toys of his own choosing, on secret hoards of liquoriced plums and on comics recounting the exploits of chivalrous swordsmen.

But his father, a widower and a maker of camphor wood chests, always expected him and his two elder brothers to risk part of their *lai-see* money on games of dice or cards. His father considered it important for each to know whether good luck of ill fortune would attend during the rest of the year. His young heart thumped when he betted. Yet, miraculously, he and his brothers always seemed to end up winning. It was not till he was nine or ten that he discovered his father had manipulated the games to ensure that each child began the year on a propitious note.

That discovery came as a disappointment. If the New Year games could be fixed, then winning did not really indicate whether a person was favoured by fortune. He wanted to find out if he had luck, so he conducted tests by systematically wagering with classmates on the outcome of examination results, football matches and other events. The results were inconclusive. They left him hankering for a way of harnessing luck.

Though luck might not always favour him, his father did. Because he did not share the dull, artisan faces of his brothers, he was not required to leave school at fourteen to learn woodcarving and carpentry. Instead his father encouraged him to aim for a career in commerce or one of the professions. Shortly after completing his secondary education, however, his father died and the prospect of a more dazzling future died with him.

The family business, together with the building from which it was conducted, was left to be shared equally among the brothers. Since he had not mastered a craft, it was agreed after much to-ing and fro-ing that he should assume responsibility for supervising stocks, purchasing materials and keeping track of orders and accounts.

Following a family tradition, each son drew an inadequate salary, mainly to dampen excessive wage expectations among *fokis* and apprentices. Shortfalls for the owners were made good through a confidential quarterly sharing of profits.

Times were changing, however. Camphor wood chests, no matter how beautifully carved or inlaid with semi-precious stones, were losing their appeal. People wanted more functional ways of storing quilts and winter clothing in their progressively smaller flats. The only steady demand, ironically, came from departing foreigners seeking to take home some memento of the East.

Quite apart from a dwindling income, Pao also became bored with his unchallenging work. It left him frequently restless for a creative outlet. He could feel neither the pleasure of working with a piece of seasoned wood nor the satisfaction of executing a well-carved composition. Indeed, the pungency of camphor wood gradually became an irritant. The dust and wood shavings in the workshop grew more intolerable by the day.

He wanted to strike out on his own, particularly when he sensed his brothers resenting his less onerous duties. But he lacked both capital and marketable skills. His bachelor status, however, dulled the edge of urgency. He allowed matters to drift, seeking diversions in *mah-jong* games and in punting on the amateur horse races organized by the Royal Hong Kong Jockey Club. Both activities soon became regular pastimes.

At the age of twenty-two he married Lai-ching, a cheerful and comely girl who had been a former classmate. They honeymooned in Macau, that indolent cross between a down-market Monte Carlo and an erratically administered Casablanca. The territory's dated charm, with hints of the Mediterranean, was novel and soothing. To crown the sojourn they won five thousand dollars at baccarat in one of its many casinos. That represented a veritable fortune and they both took it as an auspicious start to their union.

Lai-ching's father, a head clerk in a firm of solicitors, had offered as dowry a tiny flat in Causeway Bay which he had acquired through a timely foreclosure. There the couple settled down to married life. They yearned for many sons but Lai-ching soon gave birth to a daughter. Two years later, another daughter arrived. Then life began to unravel.

Rising overheads and declining sales had reached a point where Pao's share of the profits proved inadequate to bridge the gap between salary and outgoings. To make matters worse, he began encountering a run of bad luck. The cost of raising another child, particularly a daughter, seemed an imposition.

He concluded that Heaven must be frowning upon him. His father had sired three sons. His brothers had produced sons. Yet he had only daughters and could not even afford a further try for a son.

One day an idea occurred to him. It came to him like a revelation and he threw himself into developing it with all the enthusiasm of a schoolboy plotting a prank.

His years of following horse races had enabled him to spot an anomaly in the tote rules. The tote always paid three place bets, even in a field of four runners, and the minimum return on a place bet of five dollars was five dollars and ten cents. That rendered punting for a place on the favourite a virtual betting certainty. If one had sufficient capital, a two percent return in as many minutes was money for jam!

There was usually plenty of cash at the workshop to pay for raw materials, wages and other contingencies. Since races took place on Saturday afternoons, borrowing the money for a couple of hours would leave no one the wiser. When a four-horse race next appeared on a card, he took everything he could lay his hands on and betted it on the favourite to place. The horse duly obliged and he won a sum amounting to more than half a month's salary.

He was so exhilarated by his success that he could not help telling Lai-ching. But far from being pleased, she became upset.

"How can you take money that does not belong to you?" she asked. "What if something went wrong?"

"Nothing can go wrong. It's ironclad," he replied. "Besides, I haven't taken anybody's money. I've merely borrowed it for a few hours. No one is being hurt. I'm doing it for the children. How else are we to give them a decent education on what I'm making? Just take the winnings and start an education fund for them."

Lai-ching grudgingly acquiesced. During the next two seasons he made successful punts on no fewer than eight occasions. It seemed he had at last found a way of creating his own luck.

On the ninth occasion, however, disaster struck. The favourite bled during the race and had to be pulled up, leaving it unplaced. The loss suffered came to more than six times the accumulated winnings of the two previous seasons.

Pao fished a packet of cigarettes out of his pocket, lit one and blew a cloud of smoke into the cool night air. There was not another soul on the darkened deck and the steady droning of the engine sounded like the chanting of a dirge. He recalled the adage that those venturing frequently into wild mountains were bound, sooner or later, to encounter a tiger. He had encountered a tiger all right and it was devouring his life!

There was no alternative to confessing his misappropriation. He had expected brotherly understanding, forgiveness and a chance to make amends. Instead, his brothers berated him in front of the *fokis*.

"Father always thought you better than us, too bright to get hands dirty," his eldest brother yelled, his face contorted with anger. "We've been carrying you for years. This is how you repay us!"

"You've disgraced the family," his second brother added. "Who knows how much you've been stealing from us? No wonder profits are dropping. We're finished with you. We want you out."

The accusations pierced his heart. It stunned him to discover that thirty years of shared existence counted for nothing when it came to dollars and cents.

The brothers demanded that he made up the loss by signing over his third of the business, including the title to the workshop building. Otherwise they would go to the Police. He complied, tumbling in one fell swoop from being a part proprietor in a going concern to an unemployed pariah, too ashamed to show his face before kith and kin.

His resentment against his brothers brewed slowly into hatred, particularly when the value of the workshop land climbed with the colony's building boom. But hatred was a luxury he could not afford. Deprived of income, his need for employment was acute. He eventually landed a job as a clerk in a small trading firm. The salary fell far short of his family's needs, particularly when his elder daughter was ready to begin school. But he had brought his family to such a pass and he felt it incumbent upon him to find a solution.

It so happened he knew a commission agent working for shops catering to the tourist trade. A passable living could be had by hustling strangers in the streets to persuade them to purchase made-to-order suits, shirts or shoes. He arrived at arrangements with a number of shops and began roaming the streets after his normal work. It was a small step to go from touting for tailors and leather merchants to touting for girlie bars and whores. Indeed, the latter proved easier along the neon-lit streets around Fenwick

Pier, particularly with visiting servicemen. The money was certainly better.

He did not have the heart to tell Lai-ching what he was up to. To explain his absences he told his wife he had found a congenial *mah-jong* club and was spending his evenings there.

"How can you think of *mah-jong* at a time like this?" Lai-ching demanded. "you're like a stranger who only sleeps here. The children hardly see you. You're moody and irritable with them."

"I bring money home, don't I? Can't a man have a bit of fun?" he retorted. But he felt guilty. Confessing the truth would only add humiliation without bring financial relief.

"What if you lose? What if luck went against you? Your pay is barely enough to live on as it is."

"Everybody wins sometimes and loses at other times. I'm winning big and losing small, playing with suckers who are nowhere in my class. We're living no worse than before. What have you to complain about?"

Lai-ching continued to complain, however. She loathed to see him growing thin and haggard. Her mother and sisters were also starting to drop hints about the unwisdom of allowing husbands too long a leash.

Life gradually became intolerable. The punishing hours, the nights on the streets, the endless calumnies and, most of all, the crackle of tension around the home, depressed Pao beyond endurance. He had not wagered a single dollar since the debacle at the races and yet no one could think of him as anything but a gambling addict. He even had to trade on that reputation to explain his absences. He longed for a way to redeem himself, to snatch his life back from that pitiless tiger of misfortune.

One day an acquaintance told him of a small manufacturer of wigs seeking a partner. There was a fad in the United States for wigs made with human hair. Profit margins were high and the manufacturer needed fresh capital to expand.

Pao had heard of the craze and saw it as an opportunity for a fresh start. But where was he to find the capital to participate?

Suddenly he thought of Macau. During his honeymoon he could do no wrong at baccarat. If he could repeat that run of luck he would be home and dry. So on an impulse he begged and borrowed all he could and took off for the Portuguese enclave.

Luck was not with him, however. He lost all he had, leaving him in a deeper hole than before. If he settled his debts at the end of the month he would have nothing to bring home. To confess to gambling and losing in a casino would damn him forever in the eyes of the woman he loved. He had nothing even worth pawning. All he possessed was a cheap quartz watch and a ferry ticket home.

As he pondered his dire circumstances, a neatly dressed stranger of about his own age approached him. "No luck?" he asked, in a sympathetic tone of voice.

Pao shook his head.

"One needs plenty of ammunition to tussle with a casino," the stranger observed. "Staying power, that's the key. You have to stay long enough for luck to turn. If you're looking for a loan, maybe I can help."

Pao realized the stranger was a hustler for a loan-sharking syndicate. One part of his brain warned against getting involved but another part held out the hope of recovery. Before he knew it, he asked: "What's the interest?"

"Depends on how much you want and for how long," the stranger replied.

"Let's say five thousand for a couple of days, till I get back to Hong Kong. I own a factory making camphor wood chests."

"Ten per cent per month, one month's interest in advance."

"That's steep!"

"Hey, Friend, what's ten per cent for a chance to recover? You're a gambler. You know how things go. Could end up with a fortune. On the other hand, if Lady Luck doesn't smile on you, I have to send people to Hong Kong to collect. That costs money."

A sudden recklessness possessed Pao. Without further ado he accepted a loan and surrendered his travel documents as security.

After two feverish days of playing, his loan too was gone. He was escorted home by two young toughs with orders to collect.

When he got home, he found Lai-ching in a state. "Where've you been?" she cried. "You've disappeared for days! Your office said you didn't show for work. I thought something terrible had happened."

"Something terrible has," he replied. "Need five thousand dollars quickly. Please go to the bank and take it from the children's education fund."

"No! Can't touch that money. Why do you need so much?"

"Gambled in Macau and lost, if you must know!" he shouted, with unreasoning irritation. "Borrowed from a loan-shark and if I don't repay there'll be trouble."

"You got yourself into this, you can get yourself out. I'm not going to let you touch the education fund. There's little enough there as it is."

"I'll pay it back, for heaven's sake! Try and understand. If I don't pay right away, the interest will mount so fast the debt can never be cleared. We'll be in hock for life. Stop paying and the loan-shark will hurt you and the girls. He's got two men outside right now. Believe me, this is the only way. While you're at it, draw something extra for housekeeping. I won't have money for you this month."

Lai-ching gave him a look as cold as marble. Without uttering a word she made ready to go to the bank. Upon her return, she thrust the money at him, also without a word.

The following Sunday, Pao woke up to find that his daughters had gone to visit his parents-in-law. "Why have they gone so early?" he asked, as he settled down to breakfast.

"I want to talk to you alone," Lai-ching replied. Her eyes had a glazed, life-weary look and her mouth was tight with tension. It was as if she was overburdened with heartaches, recriminations and resentments.

Her appearance sent a pang of guilt through Pao. What had he done to the warm, guileless girl he married? It would have taken so little to make her happy. Yet that little had proved beyond him. As he waited for her to speak he felt as if his bowels were on fire.

"I can't take any more," Lai-ching said, finally. "It seems your gambling is more important than your family. I've discussed things with Father and he's advised me to seek a divorce. If you'll give me custody of the girls, I won't seek maintenance. My father can help me till I'm settled."

"Please don't do this!" Pao cried. "You don't know how I've had to live all these years. You and the girls are all I have. Stay with me. I promise there'll be no more loan-sharks."

"How can anyone believe you? You've got this gambling disease. It isn't enough that you play *mah-jong* night after night. You have to bring ruffians to our very doorstep. You'll never change."

"Just give me one more chance. I'll show you I can change," he cried, wild with despair.

Lai-ching shook her head. Determination was written on her face.

Seeing the unrelenting attitude, Pao burst into tears. He rushed into the kitchen, picked up the meat cleaver and chopped off the little finger of his left hand. He carried the severed finger into the dining-room, with blood streaming from the wound. "See! See!" he cried. "For you I'll cut off gambling as I have my finger! Please don't leave me."

Lai-ching screamed, recoiling from the bloody object dropped into her lap. She flung it away in panic and burst into tears. When she had got over her shock, she rushed to find something to staunch the bleeding, crying uncontrollably the while.

"Please believe me," Pao sobbed. "I'll never gamble again. I would rather lose all my fingers than let you down."

They wept together, clinging to each other, and something of the love they used to feel flickered back into life.

"Must get you to a hospital," Lai-ching said, tenderly, as she helped him to dress.

They got back from the hospital shortly before the girls returned from their visit to their grandparents. Lai-ching told them their father had lost a finger in an accident in the kitchen.

When the girls saw the bandaged hand, the older of the two asked if the finger had been sewn back. "I've read they can do that nowadays," she said. "That's why I want to be a doctor."

"No," Lai-ching replied. "I'm afraid we've forgotten that in our panic. It should be still here somewhere."

The girls searched for the finger and retrieved it from beneath a side cupboard.

A consensus was quickly reached that it should be preserved as a keepsake. The girls got a glass pickle jar and half-filled it with mentholated spirit. Pao made light of the episode and put the severed finger into the jar with exaggerated ceremony.

Pao took two weeks of sick leave from his day job and stayed at home. It surprised him how much his daughters had grown and how much they resembled their mother in their gentle, easy-going ways. He speculated on how wonderful it would be if they could really pursue the kind of life denied him.

But as his wound healed, he realized he was chasing dreams. Without money there could be no rosy future and no escape from his double-life. There would only be the same traps hidden beneath the same lies.

It seemed best that Lai-ching should divorce him. She was still young. Once rid of him she might find a good man to provide decently for her and the girls. He would then be spared the web of deception tightening around him like a shroud.

He waited for an opportune moment to broach the matter. He knew the best way of persuading Lai-ching to go along would be to play upon her mistaken belief about his addiction to gambling. The opportunity came one evening when Lai-ching remarked that the girls were growing up and had need to see more of their father.

"I've been a rotten husband and father," he began. "I want to do better but I can't. You're right about my gambling. It's a disease. I've tried to change but can't, no matter how many fingers are chopped off. When the urge is upon me, I can no more resist it than I can the movement of the tides. For the sake of the children, please divorce me as your father has suggested.

"I won't contest anything. I just want the girls to grow up in a normal family environment. I'll repay what I have taken from the education fund. That still won't be enough to see them through university but that's the best I can do at the moment. I'll take out double indemnity insurance, in case something happens to me."

Tears trickled slowly down from Lai-ching's eyes. "I thought we could make something together," she said, "particularly after our auspicious start. Have I disappointed you by not giving you a son? I'm sorry. A son might have made a difference."

"No, no. Not your fault," Pao said, comforting Lai-ching as best he could. "It's just Fate."

He realized all of a sudden how desperately he loved her. He quickly ended the discussion, fearful her next deluge of tears would wash away whatever remained of his resolve.

A few days later he moved into a small cubicle in a sub-divided back street tenement. Freed from financial responsibility, he resigned his office job to concentrate on touting. He proved quite successful in that dubious calling. He read tourist magazines and became quite innovative in his approach, collecting photographs of star local attractions to show to prospective targets. Needless to say, he also flashed flattering pictures of some of the women he worked for when appropriate.

Once he came across an article on the history of Macau and he cut out a paragraph from it and pasted it on a piece of cardboard as another selling aid.

The paragraph in question read: "Macau was founded in 1557 by Portuguese traders who leased the territory from China. Though consisting of only a few square miles, Macau soon acquired a reputation for being a wild and lascivious place. In the 18th Century, a Franciscan friar stated that he considered it the capital of lechery, robbery, treachery, gambling, drunkenness, brawling, wrangling, cheating and other vices. Some say little has changed in the last three hundred years."

He would show the passage to foreign tourists and say: "Plenty exciting place. You want look-see? I can show. I good guide."

Something ill-used and defeated in his bearing often elicited sympathy. It did not take long for him to twig that his best chance of hooking a customer lay among the middle-aged. Perhaps they, with dimming fires, were more anxious to savour afresh the vices listed in the paragraph.

When escorting tourists to Macau, he always encouraged them to have a flutter in the casinos. He calculated that a winning customer could be counted on for a generous tip. But such work resulted in a revival of his interest in finding a winning formula. As his customers gambled, he studied the casino games. His observations led him to conclude that the only way to win was to avoid protracted sessions and to resort to hit-and-run tactics. The trick was to time bets when that mysterious tide of chance favoured the punter.

He tested his theory and for a time it appeared to work. At least it proved successful enough for him to call on Lai-ching and the children with small presents and to repay money to the education fund.

In the meantime, Lai-ching had found employment as a cashier in a herbalist's store and, with a bit of subsidy from her father, she and the girls were getting by. She showed no sign of wanting to marry again.

Thus the years slipped by. The girls grew into adolescence. Pao hardly realized how quickly time had passed until he received an invitation from his elder daughter to attend her high school graduation. It dawned on him on a sudden that their university education still had to be provided for. His heart ached with self-reproach.

When his elder daughter told him she intended looking for a job after graduation, he put his foot down. "No!" he declared. "You were meant to study medicine and medicine you shall study, if that's the last thing I do. Apply for a place. I'll organize the finances."

After the graduation ceremony he collected his commissions and sold every possession of value. From experience he knew that whores and bar girls were often big-hearted towards to those in need. He explained his purpose and touched them for loans. When he had accumulated three thousand dollars he headed for Macau.

Upon arrival he went to one of the loan-sharks to negotiate a loan of ten thousand dollars.

"A lot of money," the loan-shark observed. "How do I know you're good for so much? Don't want any aggravation."

"Don't worry," Pao said, airily. "You've seen me around, sometimes with foreign friends. My brothers and I own a plant making camphor wood chests in Hong Kong. That's not going to walk away, is it? The land itself is worth a mint. I'll give you the address. Ask around. I've done business here before. If you don't want to deal, I'll go elsewhere."

The loan was quickly secured and that filled him with a sense of destiny, of things finally going his way. He wanted to prolong and savour the moment. Instead of heading for a casino at once, he went to the Portuguese restaurant where he and Lai-ching had dined during their honeymoon. He settled down to a leisurely meal of African chicken, a local Macanese delicacy, and a bottle of vinho verde.

The meal left him sated and mellowed. He wanted to be at his best before entering a casino. So he strolled along Senate Square and the waterfront for a while. When he eventually entered the largest casino in Macau, he picked up the money from the loan-shark and headed straight for the high-stake baccarat table.

He watched the fall of the cards for a while, waiting for a pattern he considered advantageous. When it finally came, he wagered twelve thousand dollars on the bank, calculating that on any individual hand the bank enjoyed a slight edge. When the bank obliged, he indicated with nonchalance that the entire sum should be left to ride. A collective murmur rippled among the players and spectators.

The bank obliged again and he felt invincible. All he needed was for the bank to oblige a third time and the university education of his daughters would be assured. So he asked for the accumulated winnings to ride again. The atmosphere around the table became electrifying. A number of punters rushed to follow his bet in the belief he was in luck.

The next deal turned out to be an égalité, a stand-off, and the tension around the table became almost palpable. Some punters saw it as an auspicious sign and increased their bets. Others took a different view and withdrew their wagers.

Pao knew he could walk away from the table at that point clearing a considerable sum after repaying his debt. It would not be enough to see his daughters through university but it would give them a respectable start. But some inner voice urged him to follow his destiny, to find the courage to make the gamble of his life. He obeyed without hesitation.

When the hands exposed on the green baize showed that the bank had lost by a single point, disappointed gasps and curses escaped from players and spectators alike. But Pao merely smiled and walked away.

The loan-shark followed and commiserated. "Rotten luck," he said. "Another loan?"

"No, that's enough for one night," Pao replied. "I have a ticket for the four o'clock ferry."

"All right. Our man will be there with your travel papers."

Pao pulled another cigarette out of his packet and lit it. A final smoke for the killer of dreams, he thought. He felt a sense of indifference, almost of relief. Life had been a long, cruel jest but he had managed to fix the odds after all. In an hour or so, his burly escort would awake to a surprise. So would his insurance company and his unworthy brothers when the loan-shark's henchmen turned up.

He stood for a long moment staring into the unfathomable blackness before pitching his unfinished cigarette into the sea. He heaved a deep sigh and straightened the collar of his jacket, as if he were about to make an entrance into some grand affair. He then climbed calmly over the railings and jumped.

Just before hitting the water, a thought flashed through his mind. Was his little finger still being kept in that glass pickle

The Company House

"So this is the mysterious East," John Cranshaw said to Robert Ferguson as they gazed upon the lush greens from the balcony of the Selangor Club. "It doesn't really look very mysterious, you know."

Cranshaw had an impressive public school voice, which matched his athletic build and his patrician manner. His voice had served him well over the years. Its warm, reassuring tones had taken him to heights not altogether warranted by his commercial abilities. But in the final analysis it still proved insufficient to secure for him that seat on the main board that his wife coveted.

Cranshaw himself had not been particularly anxious, regarding it only as a pleasant way of rounding off his career. He knew it was sometimes held against him that he was too much of a gentleman in dealings with both staff and customers, which was just another way of saying he was not aggressive enough. But he was unwilling to develop a hard edge or to suppress the natural inclinations of his character for the sake of a directorship.

By the time a vacancy on the main board occurred, he had already entered middle age. When the post went to someone junior to him, he accepted the decision without fuss, though his wife was much distressed. Later, when he was offered the consolation prize of replacing old Ferguson as head of the

Stapleton subsidiary in the Far East, his wife had insisted upon his accepting. So he headed for Kuala Lumpur, filled with ambivalence about having to find his feet in a foreign place so late in life.

Ferguson took a swallow of pink gin. The toll of the tropics marked his features. His brow was seamed and his skin leathery. What remained of his hair had turned grey and the bags under his eyes hung like tired remnants from a happier past. "You haven't been out this way before, have you? he asked.

"No. Never further than Athens till now."

"It's not a bad life. Company house and car, chauffeur and servants, club memberships and an expense account. It's quite a pampered exile, actually. It's a bit hard on the women, though. They feel cut off and are left without enough to do. When is your wife coming?"

"Not till later in the year, I'm afraid. She's getting our youngest daughter into boarding school." Cranshaw's open, guileless face, with its soft grey eyes, straight nose and strong chin, registered a fleeting look of sadness as he spoke. He missed his wife and children, for he was very much a family man.

Ferguson ordered another round of drinks, reflected for a moment on his retirement, and said: "I had best begin briefing you. We are market leaders in Malaysia, in everything from incandescent and diachronic display lamps to gas-discharge lamps. We are also strong in insulated cables and glands. Sales are healthy for accessories as well. We are holding our own in Singapore but the competition is tough in Hong Kong. Thailand looks like the next place with potential. You might spend some time to develop it. As for the rest of your bailiwick, you will simply have to mark time till their economies take off or their governments relax controls. We can go into all the projections in the office tomorrow. There are also one or two personnel problems but we can leave them till tomorrow.

"As to your personal arrangements, I have already put you up for membership in a couple of clubs. I assume you play golf? As I said, a car and a chauffeur go with the job. There is also a company house on the outskirts of town but I wouldn't live there is I were you."

"Is it horrid?"

Ferguson took another gulp of pink gin. "Yes and no. It's quite a handsome colonial building, with wide balconies on three sides and surrounded by extensive grounds. It also has separate quarters for servants. But it is supposed to have bad joss."

"Bad joss?"

"Yes, it's unlucky, inauspicious. I think what people mean is that it's haunted."

Cranshaw chuckled, revealing a fine set of teeth. "It is amazing, you know, how stories about haunted houses do the rounds. Someone once observed there is no chamber more haunted than the human mind."

"You may well laugh, but don't you remember what happened to Morrison, Courtney and Blain?"

A puzzled look came into Cranshaw's eyes. Something stirred in his memory. He delved into those mental pigeon-holes where he kept odd bits of Stapleton history but all he could retrieve were some vague notions of illnesses and of Blain being prematurely retired because of ill health.

"I remember Blain," he said. "He had to leave on health grounds. His wife was sick too, I think. I have an impression Morrison and Courtney also suffered some misfortune."

"Misfortune! They both died. Morrison was quite a splendid chap in his way. He had tremendous energy and foresight. When everybody was concentrating on Singapore, he saw the potential of Malaysia. So he directed his efforts here. When he had established a customer base he persuaded London to move the Far Eastern headquarters here. He argued that the move would provide expanded showroom space and cut overheads to boot.

"After he got here, he took a fancy to an old house which was on the market. The asking price was ridiculously low. He thought he was on to a bargain. So he snapped it up as a company house.

Within six months of moving in he died of a heart attack. He was only forty-six.

"Then Courtney came. He moved into the house and before a year was out he too was dead. Cirrhosis of the liver. Blain followed. A year later both he and his wife were diagnosed as tubercular. Can you imagine well-to-do English folk suffering from tuberculosis in this day and age?"

"That's really rotten luck," Cranshaw said. He remembered suddenly the bad jokes at the time about providence creating more room at the top and felt a twinge of guilt over benefiting indirectly from those misfortunes.

"I was working in the Middle East at the time," Ferguson continued. "They transferred me here to replace Blain. The poor chap warned me immediately about the house. He told me never to live in it because there was something queer going on. I must say that while helping the Blains to pack I felt quite ill at ease. I couldn't put my finger on it but I felt as if formless things were lurking around everywhere. There was no point taking risks, so I rented a flat and told London that the house was too damp for my wife's rheumatism. More than ten years have passed. I doubt if I would have lasted so long if I had lived there."

A latent Anglo-Saxon skepticism stirred in Cranshaw but he resisted the temptation to pour ridicule on his host. Instead, he asked: "So who's living there now?"

"Nobody. I use it to put up visiting firemen or customers from out of town. It stands empty most of the time, looked after by a housekeeper named Sim. She is someone you'll have to see to believe. I cannot even begin to describe her. She looks as if she belongs to a Hammer horror film. Incidentally, she is one of the personnel problems I'm leaving you with."

"What's the matter with her? Dishonest? Difficult to control?"

"Neither, really. Sim keeps the place in very good nick. It is just that she gives some of our guests the willies. She's probably also long past retirement. Nobody seems to know exactly how old she is, and she herself does not remember. She has been on the company payroll since Morrison bought the place. I did ask the personnel manager to see about pensioning her off, but he's afraid she might cast a spell on him. He says she's a bomoh."

"What's that?"

"That's a Malay word for witch or shaman.'

"Come on now, Ferguson! First there's a haunted house. Now there's a witch. Are you pulling my leg? We are electrical engineers, for heaven's sake. We are men of science. How can we subscribe to such poppycock?"

"You haven't been in the East as long as I have. Strange things do happen here. There are gods and demons we have never even heard of. Strange customs and black magic rule people's lives. After all, the scientific attitude is one of systematic doubt. Our ignorance of certain things does not mean they do not exist."

In the conversation that followed, Cranshaw learnt that Ferguson had denied Sim salary adjustments for the previous two years in the hope of provoking her to leave. But she made no fuss. She simply carried on. Such an underhanded approach grated against Cranshaw's sense of fair play and he resolved that once Ferguson was out of the way he would make amends. His skeptical turn of mind also tempted him to try out the house.

So, a week after Ferguson's departure, Cranshaw made his way there. As he entered the long driveway he noted that the building, though lacking in a distinctive national identity, represented a not unhappy blend of Western architectural concepts with indigenous designs. Its wide balconies and tall French windows suggested an interior well insulated from the scorching heat outside.

As he approached the car porch, he saw a waiting figure clad in black and wearing a strange, dark headgear. He immediately sensed something unusual about the person. It was only after he had got out of the car that he realized what an unforgettable sight Sim presented.

Despite Ferguson's warning, he was taken aback by Sim's appearance. There was a seared black pit where her right eye ought to have been and vitiligo, that disfiguring skin disease, seemed to have bisected her face into two startling colours. The upper part was in a dusky, tropical shade, the lower a bleached, blotchy white. Those two features made her appear like some macabre creature from the nether regions.

"Hallo. My name is Cranshaw. I'm Mr. Ferguson's successor," Cranshaw said, with the practised nonchalance instilled by good breeding. At the same time he extended his right hand in greeting.

Sim looked at him warily with her single eye before taking the hand. "You are welcome, Master," she said, in a voice that was low and surprisingly gentle.

"Do you mind showing me the house?"

"As you wish, Master."

As Cranshaw followed Sim through the house, he noticed she moved with an incredible lightness, as if she were a mere shadow floating over the polished timber floors. The ground floor was clean and spacious and exuded an aroma of incense. The potted plants, the rattan furniture and the wooden-bladed ceiling fans all confirmed those images of tropical houses conjured up by the stories of Conrad and Maugham. The shuttered bedrooms upstairs were exceptionally cool, but somehow the coolness seemed to convey the unsettling quality of catacombs.

By the end of the tour Cranshaw had concluded the place was quite habitable. Sim seemed an efficient housekeeper, in spite of her appearance. She knew every little defect in the house and demonstrated that she was right on top of her job. So, being satisfied with what he had seen, Cranshaw said: "By the way, Sim, I think there has been some mix-up about your salary the last couple of years. I have asked the personnel manager to make adjustments. I hope that is satisfactory."

"Thank you, Master," Sim said. Something responsive and long dormant flickered momentarily into life in her remaining eye.

"I'm getting rather tired of living in a hotel. I might move here for a while. At least until my wife arrives. Will that be a great bother for you?"

"This is an old house, Master. No one has lived here for a long time. The plumbing needs repairs. The linen, the crockery and some other items need replacing. It will not be as comfortable as a hotel."

In detecting the hesitancy in Sim's voice, Cranshaw said: "I'm not very demanding. Let me know your requirements and I'll have someone attend to them."

Several days later Cranshaw moved into the house. He settled in comfortably enough and Sim looked after him well. She prepared excellent native dishes and he became impressed by her cleanliness and industry.

But one day he caught sight of her with her headgear off. She was absorbed in burning incense and he was shocked to see that her appearance was even worse that he had allowed for. Her head was covered by tufts of grey hair and there appeared to be scars on her scalp from which no hair grew. As she crouched in her devotions, with the smoke of incense swirling around her, she looked like a demented scarecrow engaged in some bizarre rite. Although he had long dismissed talk about her being connected with the black arts, he nevertheless suddenly realized that his wife would be quite upset having someone like Sim around the house.

In the days that followed, Cranshaw wrestled with that dilemma. He was dead set against getting rid of Sim simply because of her looks. Such disfigurement had to be tragedy enough for any woman without his adding unjustly to her woes. On the other hand, he did not want his wife's first taste of life in the East to be more unsettling than necessary. The only solution that occurred to him was to follow Ferguson's lead in living elsewhere when his wife arrived. But that would represent a surrender of his principles and an evasion of the issue.

As he exercised his mind over the problem, he began to experience a creeping sense of discomfort and unease. Perhaps he had taken the whole thing too seriously or perhaps he was being irritated by an inability to devise a fair solution. In any case, he became less tolerant of the perpetual smell of incense around the house and his sleep became more fitful.

He would on occasion wake up in the middle of the night to strange sounds, like the soughing of wind, even though not a breath of air would be stirring outside. He also began having distressing dreams and nightmares, filled with the terrified screams of women and the cries of shadowy figures engaged in desperate combat. Sim's two-toned face would frequently intrude into those dreams but, most surprising of all, she would invariably appear with both her eyes intact.

The inability to find rational explanation for his nightmares bothered him. He could not understand why Sim should creep so persistently into his subconscious. He became increasingly convinced, however, that if there were really dark secrets about the house, then Sim would know about them. He thought of asking her but feared appearing ridiculous. In the end he decided to get on more familiar terms with her first.

So one evening, after Sim had served him an excellent curry, Cranshaw remarked: "This is very good, Sim. Thank you. Your English is good too. Are you Chinese?"

Sim gave a soft laugh. "I suppose I'm a bit of everything, Master," she said. "My father was Chinese, though he was suppose to have some Thai blood. My mother told me she was half Sakai and half Portuguese. But in this part of the world people like us can never be sure. I started working for British people when I was very young. So I had to learn your language."

"I must say you have learnt it very well. Did you work in this house before Mr. Morrison came?"

"Yes, Master. I have worked here for close on fifty years."

"Good heavens! That is a very long time! You must have gone through some distressing experiences. Mr. Morrison dying. Then Mr. Countney."

"Yes."

"Have you ever thought of retiring?"

"I have no family. I have nowhere to go. Is Master asking me to leave?"

"No, no, Sim. You can stay as long as you like. You look after me very well. But at your age, I thought the work might be too much for you."

"Master is very kind. I can manage."

"Did you have an accident? Your eye, I mean."

"Yes, Master. An accident. It happened a long time ago." A faraway look came into Sim's single eye, as if she were reliving some ancient horror. Her silence thereafter suggested she did not care to dwell on the matter. So the conversation lapsed.

A few evenings later, while Sim was serving dinner, the sudden cry of an owl so startled her that she dropped her serving spoon. A look of fear overtook her.

"Don't be alarmed," Cranshaw said. "It may sound repulsive but I think it's only an owl."

"I am sorry, Master," Sim said, as she retrieved the spoon. "It is a fish-owl. The Malays call it the ghost bird. Its cry is a warning of calamity."

"That must be just superstition. There are lots of owls around. If a calamity occurred each time they cried, the world would be in a terrible state indeed."

The very next day, Cranshaw noticed that an ugly plant, with some multicoloured threads tied around its pot, had been placed in his bedroom. The plant consisted of a number of stalks with small, spiky leaves. He could not identify the plant, nor did he take to it.

When he questioned Sim about it, she replied: "I put it there for you, Master. It will keep away evil."

Cranshaw recalled British superstitions about mistletoe and wood betony offering protection against the malice of demons. Obviously Sim must feel that he was in need of protection. That worried him, but he did not pursue the matter because he did not want to appear given to such superstitions. Nonetheless, he began wondering if Sim's strange initiative might be connected in some way with his disturbed sleep and his unusual dreams.

About ten days later, Cranshaw was suddenly seized by violent chest pains following a luncheon. Since he had never experienced anything like it before, and since he had no history of heart trouble, he thought he must have eaten something which disagreed with him. Being a cautious man, he got the chauffeur to take him to hospital. It was a lucky precaution, for he soon collapsed from the pain. It turned out to be a case of acute pancreatitis and he had to be placed immediately under intensive care.

During the hazy periods of his tussle with that debilitating illness, when he drifted between semi-consciousness and drugged oblivion, he seemed constantly to hear the cries of fish-owls. Nightmares of desperate struggles by shadowy shapes recurred. But they had become more terrifying because the dark settings for the struggles now appeared drenched in blood.

It was several weeks before Cranshaw was discharged from hospital. He was ordered to take a further period of convalescence. But his discomfiture around the house intensified. He felt its strange chilliness more acutely than could be accounted for by his weakened state.

As he took the breeze on the balcony, or strolled in the garden, he began pondering why an ailment supposedly common only to those who drank excessively should suddenly afflict a moderate drinker like himself. Tests had uncovered no organic cause. Could the attack really be linked in some way with the cries of the fish-owls and the mysterious history of the house? Were there really happenings in the East that Westerners could never hope to understand?

One morning, he discovered that the plant Sim had placed in his bedroom had turned yellow. When he drew this to Sim's attention she became greatly alarmed.

"Master, you must leave this house. There is much evil here. You will die if you remain."

"What are you talking about, Sim?"

"You will die, Master, like Mr. Morrison and Mr. Courtney. You must leave."

"Are you telling me that something in this house caused the deaths of Mr. Morrison and Mr. Courtney?"

"Yes. I tried to warn them but they ignored me. Their wives thought me a crazy woman. You have been kind to me. So please leave to save yourself."

"I don't understand any of this. What is in this house that can harm me?"

"Evil spirits.'

"Evil spirits? What are you talking about? Why should they harm me? What about you? After all, you have been here longer than any of us."

"I know the spirits and who they are. According to our beliefs, such knowledge protects me."

"What spirits are you talking about? What is going on in this house? I'm not going to leave till I know the truth."

A tear rolled down Sim's cheek from her single eye. She sighed. "Long ago I worked here as a maid," she began. "My husband was the gardener. The house was rented by one of your countrymen. He was quite an ordinary man, not at all the kind you link with passion and violence. But he got involved with a Malay girl from a nearby village, in the way that Europeans often do when they come East for the first time. She was a very pretty girl, and no one could blame him for being smitten.

"They started meeting secretly in a hut on the outskirts of the village. As time went by the master became more and more attached to the girl. Some said he behaved as if under a spell. He grew reckless and open about the affair. He even wanted a divorce, but his wife would not hear of it. Thus quarrels filled the house.

"Late one night, about two weeks before the master was due to return to England at the end of his tour, I had difficulty getting to sleep. Something troubled me. It was a sticky night, so I left my bed to cool myself in the garden. I remembered the night because the cries of fish-owls filled the air.

"As I walked around the house, I noticed that the kitchen door was open. That surprised me because I had closed it, as was my duty, before leaving for the night. When I went to shut it again, I heard some strange sounds. I became frightened. I thought thieves might have broken in.

"I woke my husband and told him of my fears. He told me I had better be sure. Otherwise, the master and mistress might get angry over a false alarm. My husband picked up a heavy parang he used for cutting wild grass and followed me back to the kitchen. Since I was more familiar with the house, he told me to see if anything was wrong while he stood guard outside.

"I went upstairs. The door to the master bedroom was open. The bedside lamp was on. Inside the master was holding his struggling wife down on the bed while the Malay girl pressed a pillow over the face of the mistress. I could not help crying out.

"The cry alarmed them, so I turned and ran. The Malay girl picked up a pair of scissors from the dressing table and came after me. In my fear and haste, I fell down the stairs. The girl caught up with me and began stabbing at me wildly. Some of her blows cut my head but one of them took out my eye. My screams brought my husband rushing into the room. When he saw the girl about to stab me again he swung his parang and at one stroke lopped off her head.

"Before my husband could help me out of the house, the master came charging down the stairs like a raging bull. He had killed his wife. When he saw his lover with her head cut off, he lost all control. He went for my husband and the two fought like tigers. I never knew how long they fought because I passed out. It was only later that I learnt they had both died from the wounds they had inflicted upon each other."

Sim broke suddenly into heavy sobs and covered her face with her wrinkled hands.

As Cranshaw listened to Sim's terrible tale, the meaning of his nightmares dawned on him. The fierce combats, the screams of women, the blood and the images of Sim with both eyes intact all fell into place. What he had taken to the sounds of wind in fact represented the gushing of blood. Something supernatural had transported him back in time to witness the murderous happenings of so many years ago and for the first time in his life he felt a fear of something he could not put a name to.

"Oh, you poor woman!" Cranshaw said, in a voice that betrayed an unfamiliar uneasiness. "But why should the spirits of those long dead want to harm those who had nothing to do with their tragedy?"

"Because they are still being tormented by their passions and their hatreds but are left without means to do away with one another. So they take it out on the living."

"I see. But since this house holds such terrible memories for you, why do you stay?"

"Look at me, Master. Am I the kind of woman men find attractive, even when I had both eyes? And yet I had a man who not only married me but gave up his life for me. How can I leave this place when I know his spirit is not at peace? Until it is time to join him, the least I can do is to soothe his suffering with offerings and incense."

Sim's reply filled Cranshaw with a mixture of admiration, pity and excitement. It spoke volumes about the poor woman's love and devotion. But if her explanations contained the germ of truth, then the entire rational basis of his life was being turned upside down. He recalled Ferguson's remark about the scientific attitude being one of systematic doubt and, suddenly, he began to see the Eastern chaos of castes, creeds, cultures and conflicts in a fresh light. A new universe of mystery and speculation lay before him and he knew he only had to find the courage to plunge into it to gain rewards far richer than being on the main Stapleton board in London.

"The Company House" has appeared in the *Regent* magazine in Hong Kong.

About the Author

David T.K. Wong was born in Hong Kong. Educated in China, Singapore and Australia, he acquired degrees at Stanford University and the Institute of Social Studies at The Hague. He was also a Queen Elizabeth House Fellow at Oxford University. After working as a journalist in Hong Kong, London and Singapore he joined the Administrative Service in Hong Kong. He retired as one of the most senior Chinese officers in the government before embarking on a career in commerce as the managing-director of an international trading firm based in Hong Kong.

He is the founder of the annual David T.K. Wong Fellowship in creative writing at the University of East Anglia in Britain. The Fellowship awards £25,000 to each successful candidate writing in the English language a work of fiction set in Asia. He is also the founder of an international prize for short stories run by International PEN, a writers' organization with chapters in some 150 countries. The prize is worth £7,500.

David Wong is the author of two previous collections. He is currently working on a long novel set in Hong Kong.

Orchid Pavilion Books

Orchid Pavilion Books is the literary imprint of Asia 2000 Ltd., Hong Kong publishers of quality books since 1980. The imprint is inspired by the *Orchid Pavilion Preface*, a treatise on life penned by Wang Xizhi, China's most famous calligrapher.

To quote from *Behind the Brushstrokes*, an Asia 2000 book by Khoo Seow Haw and Nancy Penrose:

> By 352 A.D., Wang Zizhi was 50 years old, his reputation as a calligrapher was well established, and he had served as a court minister for many years. In the late spring of that year Wang Xizhi invited 41 calligraphers, poets, relatives and friends to accompany him on an outing to Lan Ting, the Orchid Pavilion, in the city of Shaoxing, Zhejiang province. It was the time of the year for the purification ceremony, when hands and bodies were cleansed with stream water to wash away any bad luck. The group of friends and scholars sat on each side of a flowing stream, and a little cup made out of a lotus leaf, full of wine, was floated down the stream. Whenever it floated in front of someone, that person was obliged to either compose a poem on the spot or to drink the wine as forfeit if he failed to come up with a poem.
>
> By the end of the day, 37 poems had been composed by 25 scholars. Wang Xizhi, as the head of this happy occasion, picked up a brush made out of rat whiskers and hairs and wrote on the spot the greatest masterpiece of Chinese calligraphy, the *Lan Ting Xu*, or the *Orchid Pavilion Preface*. Written on silk in the outstanding style of *Xing Shu* (Walking Style), the composition contains 28 vertical rows and 324 words. It is a philosophical discourse on the meaning of life. Wang Xizhi's calligraphy in this work is full of a natural energy, inspired by the happiness and grace of the moment, brimming with refinement and elegance. The *Orchid Pavilion Preface* became the greatest piece of *Xing Shu* and, although Wang Xizhi later tried more than 100 times to reproduce the work, he was never able to match the quality of the original.

Quality Books   ASIA 2000   From Asia 2000

Fiction

Dance with White Clouds	Goh Poh Seng
Lipstick and Other Stories	Alex Kuo
Chinese Opera	Alex Kuo
The Last Puppet Master	Stephen Rogers
Sergeant Dickinson	Jerome Gold
The Ghost Locust	Heather Stroud
Shanghai	Christopher New
A Change of Flag	Christopher New
Chinese Box	Christopher New
Last Seen in Shanghai	Howard Turk
Cheung Chau Dog Fanciers' Society	Alan B Pierce
Riding a Tiger, The Self-Criticism of Arnold Fisher	Robert Abel
Childhood's Journey	Wu Tien-tze
Getting to Lamma	Jan Alexander
Chinese Walls	Xu Xi
Daughters of Hui	Xu Xi
Hong Kong Rose	Xu Xi
Temutma	Rebecca Bradley & Stewart Sloan

Poetry

Round — Poems and Photographs of Asia	Barbara Baker & Madeleine Slavick
Traveling With a Bitter Melon	Leung Ping-kwan
Coming Ashore Far From Home	Peter Stambler
Salt	Mani Rao
The Last Beach	Mani Rao
Water Wood Pure Splendour	Agnes Lam
Woman to Woman	Agnes Lam
New Ends, Old Beginnings	Louise Ho
An Amorphous Melody — A Symphony in Verse	Kavita

Order from Asia 2000 Ltd
Fifth Floor, 31A Wyndham Street, Central, Hong Kong
Telephone: (852) 2530-1409; Fax: (852) 2526-1107
E-mail : sales@asia2000.com.hk; Website : http://www.asia2000.com.hk